COMMUNITY CONFESSIONS

A DI Huws Crime Thriller Book 3 of 3

ANNE ROBERTS

To my family and friends who have encouraged me in my scribblings. And to my step- grandaughter for her support, and whom I couldn't do without, thank you Hayley Mitchell.

Chapter One

IT WAS NOT the best of nights in Allt Goch. Winter reluctantly stepping aside for Spring and then, without warning, hurtling back as if it had changed its mind and refusing to let its icy grip go. The intermittent squalls of driving rain had kept most of the locals in their homes that evening, open fires and log burners full to the brim and blazing like the fires of hell themselves.

The pub however was relatively busy. The Tywysog Llewellyn; hub of the village now sadly, since all other amenities except for the village hall had gone.

The same crowd visited almost nightly, sitting pints in hand, on their long-claimed seats.

Tuesday was Male Voice Choir rehearsal night, a lively bunch of men, mixed ages, joined by wives and partners to satiate their post singing thirst and hunger, it was the pub's weekly curry night. There was a different theme each night, which was welcomed as takeaways for some or a cheap, filling meal for the culinary-challenged regulars.

The chat was raucous, on occasions bawdy, depending on the level of inebriation. Bass voices booming their various arguments, an answer following in a higher-pitched tenor tone.

It never became particularly heated, the presence of 'other halves' keeping tempers on an even keel.

Hard to imagine that less than an hour before, the majority of the clientele would have been belting out old Welsh hymns and popular songs.

By nine-thirty, some had left, unwilling to risk the chance of a sore head the following day, in many of their cases a workday. They walked briskly to their nearby homes, coat collars pulled up against the wind and rain.

Michael the landlord had not been at his position behind the bar very long, having attended an incredibly dull and unproductive community council meeting. The never-ending winter, creating a distinct lack of enthusiasm in the quorum that had been present that evening.

He knew all the locals and worked hard at his banter to welcome newcomers that ventured in. Always a welcome to be found in his pub for any waifs and strays, with the coal fire blazing at one end of the big lounge. He kept the music system low to allow the lads to listen to whichever football game happened to be playing on the large screen telly in the corner.

It was a strange new world now, post-pandemic. Everyone who came through the doors had to show their Covid-19 vaccination passport in order to partake in normal life. Most, apart from the few that remained reluctant, did so willingly. Those that didn't were not allowed in.

The door opened, wind funnelling through, blasting the main bar area in a chill unwelcome wind, coat collars pulled together by the lads at the bar, who glared at the incomers as if they had brought the wind with them on purpose. Everyone settled back pretty soon and continued their banter. March had just given way to April; the clocks had changed. April fools jokes had no doubt been played just that morning, so it was surprise and laughter that met the next person to barge unceremoniously through the door hardly able to catch his breath.

"There is a bloke just down the road, crawling along virtually on all fours covered in blood, I told him I would go for help, can someone phone an ambulance, I have no signal at all on my phone".

He turned on his heels and left as abruptly as he entered, leaving the inhabitants of the bar just looking at each other in disbelief, open-mouthed, pints suspended midway between bar and lips.

The first to take action was Michael the landlord, well-used to emergencies in his voluntary role as a member of the local Coast-guard team. He was followed through the door by a couple of the choir members, not necessarily medically trained, but local young farmers, practical and capable, but more used to sick sheep and cattle than humans.

The door closed out the wind, chatter resumed, a trawl of people from the lounge bar wondering what the shouting had been about, a couple grabbing their coats to go to assist while the rest just refilled their pint glasses.

Chapter Two

THE PERSON who raised the alarm was heard shouting from the direction of the back road out of the village, encouraging them to quicken their pace to help.

Into view quickly came the vision of a man on all fours with another man next to him.

Michael was first up to him, his well-trained brain, already taking in the scene around them for fear of any further danger. He dropped to his knees alongside the casualty, by the amount of blood leaving his body in multiple places, casualty would be putting it mildly.

"What's your name mate?" Michael saw immediately that the young man was in a bad way, pale beyond pale, lips taking on a dangerously blue tinge, gasping, open-mouthed with every slow noisy breath. He put his ear down to him in an attempt to hear the words that were disappearing on the wind as they left the young man's mouth. "Simon, Sssimon," he gasped.

"What can we do?" shouted the person nearest to Michael.

"Phone 999 again, tell them we have a casualty with serious injuries. Serious. Does anyone have the What 3 words app on their phone or even an ordinance survey grid reference?"

"Yes I have, I'm always out in the middle of nowhere on my tractor, my wife got told about it on a first aid course she did at work, hang on," responded one of his farmer neighbours.

The location was found, the call was made. The rain joined the wind, hammering down like the proverbial stair rods, illuminated by the single solitary street light that lit the scene with an eerie orange glow.

"Hold the phone to my ear," demanded Michael once the location had been given.

"Male, probably mid-twenties, I've not assessed him fully yet, but he has some serious blood loss, from what I can make out, multiple locations. His breathing is slow and struggling, laboured, way below normal stats now and his level of consciousness and response is diminishing by the minute. I'll do what I can, but please hurry."

At the end of the call, Michael shouted at the other people present to return to the pub and bring him the first aid kit and as many bar towels as they could grab.

"Be as quick as you can," he ordered as he tried his best to press with his bare hands on the worst points of bleeding.

Two men left to do his bidding. At this point, the young man gave a gurgle and fell forwards onto the ground, his attempts to get in enough air by crawling on all fours now too exhausting for him.

Michael, as gently as he could, turned him onto his back, "Keep an eye on his breathing, let me know straight away if it changes, keep talking to him, keep checking that he is still responding, even if it's just a grunt, it's important." This comment was directed at Eddie the local postie who took up a position at the young man's head.

Michael was by now tearing the young man's shirt with his bare hands, buttons popping, the sight that befell him was an unbelievable number of small round random holes in his abdomen and ribcage.

"Jesus Christ what the fucking hell has happened to you?" asked Michael, shocked at the sight, then remembering his training regretted pointing out to the casualty just how injured he in fact was.

No response was forthcoming. Nothing.

"Are those stab wounds?" asked one of the lads knelt opposite him.

"I've never seen stab wounds, except for First-Aid courses, but I can't imagine they can be anything else, can you?"

Multiple feet were running towards them now, the towel gatherer having by his haste and panic alerted the remaining beer drinkers that there was actually some sort of drama going on.

Michael grabbed at the nearest towel and pressed it onto the lad's abdomen, covering at least two bleeding holes. He indicated for another man to do the same, in another area.

"There is blood pouring out under him too," declared another bystander. "I can see it running onto the road."

"OK, give me a hand to get him in a sitting position, it may help his breathing whilst I check his back," demanded Michael of no one in particular.

"For fuck sake, he looks like a colander." declared a shocked bystander.

"Well don't just stand looking, grab a towel and try to staunch some of this bleeding. Simon? You're going to be fine, don't listen to these idiots, they've had a few too many beers." Michael once again directed his chatter towards the young man.

There was no response from the casualty, by now drifting off into unconsciousness as he leant against the kneeling figure of Eddie behind him.

"Where the hell is the ambulance?" shouted a woman who had joined the macabre scene, doing her best to shelter the casualty with her pink umbrella, creating a surreal vision on a rural road through the village, in the light of the nearest lamp post, rain washing the young man's life blood away, to run down to the nearest drain, people stepping aside to avoid staining their shoes.

"I think I can hear a siren," volunteered one spectator, likely pleased that they could at least be the bringer of some positive news to the party.

"Can you hear him breathing?" shouted Michael at Eddie at the casualty's head, fully supporting his weight against his own legs and chest.

"I'm not sure, there is too much noise for me to be able to hear anything much."

"Shut up for a minute everyone," ordered Michael loudly, he placed his palm gently on the lad's chest and his ear near to his face.

"Shit, he's arrested, lay him down flat, let's get some chest compressions started. Anyone done this before? Anyone?"

Not one response. Michael had already started, all his energy directed at his task.

"Phone 999 again," he demanded of anyone that would listen, "tell them he has arrested and to get a move on."

By now another young man was on his knees opposite him, ready to take over.

"I've only ever done this on a course at work."

"Great, son, thank you. Are you ready to take over for a couple of minutes? Copy where my hands are and keep pushing down hard and fast. Just do your best."

He placed his hands on the young man's chest, mirroring Michael's position then he hesitatingly began pressing down, looking at a nodding Michael for reassurance and encouragement.

"Go on, a bit harder, that's great," encouraged Michael.

This grim scene was being watched by a small crowd that had migrated from the pub, not to help, just to watch, almost as if they were watching a television programme playing out before them. There was no doubt though that any one of them would have stepped up to the plate and jumped to any task that they were asked. They just needed directing.

"They're here," came a shout "Watch out folks, the ambulance is here, let it come through."

People moved aside but were still within viewing distance. The villager, who had alerted them of the incident in the first place had clearly popped to his nearby home and gathered a couple of decent hand-held lamping torches, illuminating the area. Another had breathlessly arrived with the village hall defibrillator.

The paramedics immediately set to their task of doing everything within their control, Michael continued with the chest compressions whilst one paramedic, straight away placed their own defibrillator pads on the casualty's chest whilst the second, carefully placed a tube down his throat. Within a couple of seconds, the shout to 'stand clear' was heard as the defibrillator fired a shock, but to no avail.

Michael was asked to continue his compressions as an attempt was made to insert a line into the crook of the arm, the once-pounding blood vessel now flat as a ribbon.

A second attempt was made in the wrist, successful this time. A bag of fluid was attached and the tallest spectator present, chosen as a drip stand, an order to push the fluid through made loudly by the kneeling paramedic. The spectator, pushed to a position of responsibility that was a little beyond his level of confidence, took the clear fluid-filled bag in both hands and gently squeezed, whilst the paramedic adjusted the flow wheel to his satisfaction.

A look at the defibrillator and a pre-measured vial of adrenaline was drawn up into a syringe and administered through the port in the drip line, still to no response. The young man had rapidly changed from pale to a distinct tinge of blue, clear to be seen in the torch light, he was dying right there in front of his audience. A couple had the astonished look of rabbits caught in headlights. They would have nightmares about this, no doubt about it.

A second crew arrived, one member relieving Michael of his chest compressing duty. Michael recognized with some despair that were no longer shocking him, he knew this was not a good indicator of the outcome, but he gladly left the experts to their work.

Michael realised how wet and cold he had now become, the levels of adrenaline that had minutes ago coursed through his body now receding rapidly. Well, used to incidents, but normally better prepared, and kitted out in his coastguard togs. Now it caused him to tremble as he stood back taking in the scene. The spectators had now descended into a shocked silence, a few female sobs could be heard disappearing on the wind.

He told the paramedic that they had no information whatsoever on the casualty, other than that his name was possibly Simon, as it had been the only word he had been able to say. Apparently, he had appeared out of the darkness crawling along the road from somewhere, literally full of holes, just bleeding out, he could not possibly have come far in that state.

"The police are on their way, they won't be long, I suggest you and everyone else here, goes back into the pub to get yourselves warmed up, and on behalf of our casualty, thank you all very much for trying to help him." The paramedics took a few minutes to make sure that all their equipment, and detritus had been cleared away and the lone responder fetched a blanket from his car to cover the young man, presumably unable to now move him until the police had been.

Michael heard the dreaded declaration of 'life extinct' and the noting of the time of death as he looked on, knowing now that this was more than likely a crime scene.

Allt Goch once again the location of a terrible crime. What on earth had this close-knit little village done to deserve all this? He was followed by a small band of people as he made his way back to his pub, each one subdued and silent. Michael went straight upstairs to change and compose himself, whilst no doubt, the others described the scene in gory detail to anyone else that would listen in the bar downstairs.

He doubted from the start that the young man would live. Too much blood loss and probably serious internal injury as well as the obvious external damage. He shook his head at the thought of more deaths in the area. It had been a sad few years. Another loss for a family somewhere.

He was just about to make his way downstairs after a brief sit down in his upstairs lounge, when his phone rang, his landline. All his friends and even his accountant used his mobile, his heart fell as he predicted who the caller was.

The Police.

"Yes, that's right, I'm the landlord. Myself and a group of people were there this evening," he paused to listen a moment before continuing.

"Oh, I'm so sorry to hear that, but I suspected it would be the case. He was in a pretty bad way when he was found."

Clearly, the voice on the phone was not party to the fact that he had heard the paramedic declare the young man's death.

Another pause, a questioning look appearing on his face. "The person who came in to tell us is a local, yes," he answered.

"No, he's definitely a good guy. Born and bred here and lives nearby, I've known him for years. He stayed and did what he could to help, he even went home and got his hunting torches, or whatever he uses them for." He shook his head at the next question.

"Well, yes, he does have a gun, he deals with foxes locally for farmers. No, I don't think he was in any way involved, he isn't that sort of bloke, I'll vouch for him being a decent chap, as would everyone else sitting in the bar at this moment. In fact, he's down there amongst them, like the rest of us, pretty shaken. OK, thank you officer, I'll persuade the ones that were involved to stay until you arrive, but I do know some will already have gone home, a couple were pretty shocked by it all. They are all reasonably local to the village though, so we will be able to give you contact details."

He put the phone down and sighed as he closed the lounge door behind him.

Michael descended his stairs, opened the dividing door between the pub kitchen and the bar, and sensed a very subdued atmosphere to what it had been just an hour earlier, though he admitted to himself, it felt a lifetime.

"Heads up folks," he rang the time bell, producing grunts of complaints from some, but a huddle had already formed in a corner, of those who had witnessed the tragedy.

The news that the police were en-route to take statements was met with a few grumbles which immediately quietened in response to Michael's offer of a drink on the house to steady their nerves, and an offer of a pen and some paper to quietly write down their individual parts in the incident, in case they got intimidated later by the presence of the police, or too inebriated, not that he voiced this latter worry. He would keep an eye on them.

He told them at this point, that the young man had actually passed away on the roadside.

There were mutterings and shakes of the head as they lined up at the bar for their free drink of choice. No doubt, Michael expected, the most expensive they could find. Regular beer drinkers would most definitely be ordering brandy or whisky.

At this point in time, he was not in the mood and really did not care, there were no hesitations or refusals on his part.

Chapter Three

BY THE NEXT morning even the reluctant pub attendees had all given their individual statements late into the previous night. Nothing particularly enlightening or incriminating had been said. Witness statements were written down by officers, listening to various degrees of unnecessary drama, of what had been seen and done the night before.

The road from the pub out of the village had quickly been closed off the previous night by the forensics team. Cars having to take a narrow back loop road in order to navigate the closure.

The terrace of houses adjacent to the incident had all been visited as enquiries were made regarding any suspicious movements the night before. Inhabitants were prevented temporarily from leaving their houses for fear of contaminating any evidence, which in this case meant they were trapped by their location unless the more desperate climbed their rear garden walls and went through the fields. A fair few did. Mostly to make their way to the pub.

· · ·

No one seemed particularly perturbed by their temporary imprisonment, some behaving as if it was indeed the most exciting occurrence in their lives, curtains twitching, phones hot with conversation and conspiracy theories, social media on fire, and still the young lad lay in a crusting congealing pool of blood just yards from their front doors in a white crime scene tent. Coveralled and masked forensics officers were seen going in and out of the structure with various plastic evidence bags clutched in their hands.

It seems the wind and rain had masked any sounds the previous evening. Clearly an injured young man crawling on all fours past their front doors had neither been seen nor heard. Any cries for help not loud enough to rise above the telly or the gusting wind.

Teams of extra officers were rapidly being drafted in at the Anglesey police base in Llangefni, all prepared as soon as it got light enough to take part in a strictly structured grid search, inch by inch of the road and common. The dog teams would also be working alongside them when they eventually arrived from Cheshire. It would be a hard few days' work considering that once out of the village, they were going to be combing acre upon acre of common land.

Uniformed police stood guard to prevent any onlookers from infringing on the area. A couple of onlookers could be seen sheltering in the porch of the pub. More daytime drinkers than normal had entered the doors, no doubt all with their ideas on what had happened and speculating on who had carried out this awful crime on their doorstep. A majority just fishing for gossip.

· · ·

Within a short time, as more officers were arriving on scene, a black transit van with Private Ambulance written discretely but nonetheless obviously, on the side panel, arrived to take the body away, the initial forensic investigation on-scene now concluded.

Chapter Four

"HEY, LONG TIME NO SEE IDRIS," stated Emyr Rowlands the local pathologist as DI Huws stepped into the autopsy suite. "I thought you had about done your thirty by now and was preparing to enjoy your retirement with our Jane." He winked cheekily.

"Don't you dare whisk her away from me any time soon, she's the best assistant I've ever had the luck to work with. Well trained; reads my mind even. Anyway, isn't it time you let your young side-kick Justin here take over? I'm sure he'll make a smashing DI."

Justin Howard acknowledged the compliment with a smile which made a very rare appearance these days.

"I wish. I was actually due to enjoy my retirement do at the end of this week, but the DCI phoned this morning to say they had a suspicious death last night, a young man who I believe is lying in your fridge as we speak, and yes, I agree DS Howard here will make a superb job of it, when he gets to step into my shoes. As for Jane, well-"

He tapped the side of his nose in a mixture of ' who needs to know' and a 'mind your business', with a wide grin on his face.

They both went up the short flight of stairs to the viewing room, a far cry from his first ever experience of an autopsy room, the likes of Howard here had no idea how much better it now was, and no doubt was fed up of him going on about it every time they had need to attend.

He had become fond of the lad after his awful loss the year before, even feeling a little fatherly towards him and keeping an eye, all very professional of course. He felt pleased that Howard looked upon him as someone to turn to in need. He had promised him a week's holiday, walking together, but as yet Justin had claimed not to be in the right frame of mind to accompany him on a hillwalking jaunt.

Most certainly his experience and capability in the job had come on in leaps and bounds, his man-management skills improving, gaining a lot of respect from the team. A definite one to take his place, when he, eventually was allowed to retire from his post. One last job the DCI had said, one last job.

He took a seat and fiddled in his pocket, for a mint imperial, something fresh in his mouth, a bit of a bounce back to the Vicks up the nose days of old to disguise the smell. Though being in a glass-fronted gallery there never was any. He tapped his sides, not finding the sweets, then realising they were in another pocket. He still hadn't got used to his new coat, purchased for him by Jane on his recent birthday as a replacement for his old Mackintosh, that she said made him look like a slightly taller version of Columbo and equally dishevelled. Well, that was her reasoning anyway. They had enjoyed a few outings together in the last six months or so, nothing too serious, both had hated the idea of 'dating' at their stage in life, preferring a walk followed by a meal, then a sit down in comfy slippers watching a film, with a cup of tea.

He was happy to do it this way. His old mum seemed pleased. His daughter Elin, on the other hand was still less than enthusiastic but no doubt she would become more accepting over time. Jane always left at the end of the evening for her own comfortable flat. Or vice versa if he was at Jane's. It suited them both.

The part that thrilled him the most was that his old mum had agreed to return to her own home, claiming that if he had someone who might take on the responsibility of looking after him she would be happy.

He had not admitted yet that Jane had in no way agreed to do his washing and ironing, but he would get by.

Still, on occasion, he felt a pang of guilt, guilt about being happier, guilt about a developing relationship, when Gwen had barely been gone two years, and guilt that he felt that he was betraying their 19-year-old daughter's memories of her mother.

He smiled as he fished two fluff-covered mint imperials out of a pocket, passing one to Justin who at a glance at the offerings, raised his hand and politely declined.

Huws placed both in his mouth and settled into his seat, knowing that young Howard would do a fine job of any note-taking that needed doing. Justin looked across at him, the quietness of the room disturbed by loud crunching.

Emyr Rowlands, as professional as ever, included them both in all the detail. Declaring that in front of him was a young male, possibly, by a look at his teeth, and an experienced once over, estimated to be around his mid-twenties. Fit-looking and lean, no spare flab on him anywhere.

The young man had clearly looked after himself, on first evaluation he suggested that death had been caused by multiple stab wounds which had penetrated a number of internal organs which he would have a better idea of as the autopsy progressed.

Jane was at his side with her camera, recording all that was pointed out to her by her senior, so at ease and fluid in her movements, as she moved around the body, her experience was obvious.

Jane and Rowlands between them were clearly counting the puncture holes in the body, the front, and on turning him on his side, the puncture wounds around his buttocks and upper thighs. Sixteen individual holes in all. He inserted some closed long narrow scissors into a couple of the holes, and with some horror, Huws saw that the complete instrument bar the finger holes disappeared into the punctures.

Rowlands painstakingly inserted the scissors into each hole measuring the depth against a surgical tape measure held up for him by

Jane, they repeated this with each hole, she wrote the measurement down on a completed diagram of the victim's front and back.

Some of the holes he described as narrow in circumference, no more than a third of an inch. But between nine and ten inches deep, the inches Huws knew perfectly well were for his benefit, Rowland knowing that his old friend was still very much better able to imagine sizes in inches and feet, than centimetres. Old school.

The speaker in the viewing gallery went quiet, Emyr Rowlands and Jane seemingly measuring the distances between the puncture holes.

They almost look like air gun pellet holes said Jane as their voices became audible again. However, declaring on the next breath that they would unlikely have penetrated to those depths, unless they were delivered from a very, very close range. Rowlands stood back and turned to a computer behind him and tapped something in that Huws could only just see. He was on Google!

"Good God Rowlands, are you actually Googling a cause of death?" asked Huws with a hint of irreverence, that he most certainly did not mean with any malice.

"Well, not quite, I'm looking up pronged tools. I'm coming to the rapid conclusion by the positioning of these punctures, that they may well have been inflicted in pairs but by one weapon, and likely one perpetrator."

"Really?" asked Howard. "What sort of tool?"

It became apparent to Huws that Howard was also himself Googling on his phone.

"Here's a likely weapon, a pitchfork," announced Rowlands. It seems that the prongs are between nine and twelve inches long and are set at a width of around six or seven inches apart. That seems to fit the bill with these injuries, and by the looks of things, pushed in with a force that in places they have gone right up to the hilt."

Huws shook his head in disbelief.

"Unbelievable, who the hell would do this sort of thing, it doesn't bear thinking about."

" Well, it isn't my job to find that out, but I would suggest you ask a few local farmers, not that I lay the blame at their door, but it is quite an old-fashioned tool to use now in this modern age of mechanisation and big bales, but it was the tool of choice at one time for picking up and lifting small bales onto a hay trailer. I used to help my grandfather do that on his farm as a young boy. I can't imagine it is used for much else these days, but no doubt every farmer will still have one hanging around in a shed. The other thing about the weapon is, that it was very rusty, there are significant flakes of rust on the edges of some of these holes as the prongs have been plunged in and pulled out."

He continued. Idris Huws was aghast, he had seen a fair few things in his career, but this was just another level of horrific.

"If on the basis that it is a double-pronged tool then our sixteen wounds become eight individual efforts to inflict significant damage. Whoever did this most certainly meant to do serious harm, they certainly meant to kill.

I will also maybe offer the opinion, that this young man may well have been carrying a rucksack by the positions of the wounds, as it may well have provided him with some protection. Quite likely two initial wounds executed from behind and six carried out with the young man facing his attacker, who certainly meant business.

I find it amazing that he seems to have escaped and made his way into the village.

Have you followed a trail of blood?"

Howard responded that indeed that task was no doubt already underway.

Rowlands declared at the end of his initial report that as it was quiet, and no queue for his services, that they would break off for a cup of tea, as his internal examination was likely to be complicated and without doubt would take a very long time to do the job accurately and thoroughly.

He was unsure whether they might even find that the top two holes in his lower back may well indeed be exit holes from two of the puncture wounds at the same level on his abdomen. He was lean enough in his midriff area that a nine, ten-inch spike may well have gone through completely front to back. Piercing through some pretty vital organs on their journey through.

Whatever had happened was not a quick means of killing, and no doubt the poor victim would most certainly have suffered immeasurably.

This was the work of pure evil.

Chapter Five

DS JUSTIN HOWARD left Huws to enjoy his cup of tea and a chat with both Rowlands and Jane. He. himself was rarely in the mood these days to take part in general chit chat, preferring to just get on with whatever job was in hand at the time.

He spent much, if not all of his spare time, beavering away at the Littleton case that they had dealt with the previous year. Granted, Littleton had been put away for the killing of his partner Steffan Parry, but as was feared at the time, on a charge of manslaughter as opposed to murder. This clearly made him likely to be released before the end of his imposed prison term of a measly 18 years. Thankfully it wasn't the minimum custodial sentence allowed of two years but there was a huge chance he may get parole and an early release.

Howard spent every minute trying to find enough evidence to pin the deaths of four other people on him too.

He had become less and less sociable in his work, preferring to do what he had to, but keep to himself. His life had become increasingly dark and insular. He had, much to his own disappointment found solace in the whisky bottle. Most definitely Steffan would have been incandescent with horror at finding a half-drunk bottle of whisky next to his laptop most evenings.

His friends in the job had by now given up trying to invite him to join them for an after-work pint, he was also thankful that Idris Huws had eventually stopped asking him when he would like to join him for a few days in the lakes or Scottish Highlands to do some fell or Munro walking. An idea that had been spawned when Justin was in the deepest depths of his grief. He spent his time alone in their flat going through the case with a fine-toothed comb, lest he had missed something. It was still as far as he was concerned, 'their' flat. His biggest challenge at the moment was disguising the hangover that he now endured most mornings. His companion a constant supply of paracetamol.

He chose today to drive to the scene of the crime in Allt Goch village and see if he could be of any guidance to the search teams. They were preparing to draw in a couple of the local Coastguard search teams to brief as well as a land search team based nearby.

It was strange how a small, relatively remote part of this island of Anglesey, had suffered in the last few years and that was without the ongoing Covid- 19 pandemics that continued to ebb and flow through all their lives since the beginning of 2020. He wasn't sure that it would ever really go away.

The village was relatively quiet until he reached the junction near the pub, blue and white tape still closing off the rural road out of the other end. He realised that a lot of the locals were gathered by the pub, no doubt wanting to absorb every second of the goings-on in their little village for later discussion in the pub. Two large Coastguard vehicles and one smaller one were parked to the side of the pub. A number of team members already donning their protective overalls and fluorescent jackets. These would most definitely be needed as winter was still unrelentingly whipping the wind up around their ears. Fluorescent buffs were still worn, reflecting the Covid precautions with helmets atop, goggles, and head torches at the ready should the search be prolonged. Not the easiest gear to move around in with any degree of agility and comfort imagined Howard.

Normally search teams such as these were looking for human casualties, today they were looking for absolutely anything that may make some sense of the atrocity that had befallen the young man.

Identifying him beyond the name Simon would be attempted, by the team over the next few hours, but more likely days.

Howard held his warrant card up for the attending officer then dipped under the tape that the obliging man lifted up. He was not an officer Howard recognized, but then again, a fair few had been drafted in from the mainland to help.

The blood on the road had now dried to a crust, no doubt shortly to be washed off by pressure hose. Some very gruesome things needed doing at crime scenes, as Howard was fully aware, and they needed doing with as much dignity as could be mustered by the crime-scene cleaners.

A small crowd of red-coated searchers were now gathering on the fringes of the common around a large white van, clearly, their operations base, as were a few with search trained dogs, red harnesses indicating their specialist skills.

He was aware of an officer preparing to guide everyone in their own particular search area.

The police were wellington'd and each in possession of a broom handle or at least a stick, which to Howard at least, looked very much like the average broom handle.

Instructions were given, rucksacks were heaved onto shoulders. An order to look for absolutely anything that could be connected to the young man from the previous evening.

The searchers, keen and enthusiastic, having already had to defer expertise at this point to the police search leader, were now waiting for an unfruitful search overhead by a police-controlled drone.

Before the searchers were actually allowed to start their sections, the search dogs would firstly do a sweep before any scent was tainted. This didn't take long.

Within a short time of coordinating radio channels, the crowd moved off as one, no apparent organization until they hit the common and then spread out with hardly an arms-length between them and the searcher next to them. Almost shoulder to shoulder. This search would be slow and fastidious, if also laborious and hard walking through the knee-high heather and bracken.

Jason Howard decided that at this point in the investigation his time would be best served returning to the incident room at Llangefni, which he knew would have been prepared for purpose overnight. There would not be much information there as yet, but, as with every other crime, the evidence would soon build up.

He would concentrate today on trying to get a positive ID on Simon once the photographs were available to him from the autopsy. The ever-efficient Jane would be sending them through as soon as she was able to.

Chapter Six

EMYR ROWLANDS and Jane were back at work, DI Idris Huws having returned to the viewing room, already regretting that he hadn't used the break to fetch a sandwich from the WRVS shop in the main hospital building. His hunger pangs would have to wait though as he had been warned that this procedure may well take a fair bit of time.

Rowlands was following autopsy procedure to the absolute guidelines, but was less concerned with the head and skull area, concentrating instead on the trunk. Normally a clean incision would be made to expose the internal organs after sawing down through the chest.

He explained that he wanted to take particular care with the abdominal organs since he needed to see which organs had been affected by the weapon and discover whether there was one major bleed or multiple sources.

Rowlands worked precisely and carefully, more akin to a surgeon than a pathologist. Huws remembered how Rowlands had once said a pathologist was an expert at taking bodies apart whereas a surgeon was skilled at putting them together again. Though Huws knew that his old friend was pretty good at the reconstruction too, something he did immense care and dignity. That is what Huws liked; the dignity.

The skin was carefully drawn away from the abdomen, divided from the underlying membrane slowly and meticulously, Rowlands noting each puncture as he went along. Jane recorded each movement with the camera, moving around the table to follow Rowland's skilled scalpel work. The first puncture he lined up with another in a horizontally paired stab. The right-hand side of the body had a direct strike through the middle lobe of the liver, though liver being the texture it was had all but completely closed the pathway through towards its dorsal side. The left-hand prong had nicked the right side of the spleen.

Rowlands declared that these injuries alone would have caused him to bleed out eventually.

He started work on another pair which he declared to be at a slight angle, one prong having entered between the eighth and ninth rib and penetrated the pleura around the lung which would have allowed air into the chest cavity, causing progressive deterioration in the victim's breathing, the other prong being lower had the bottom of the spleen.

Painstakingly, he worked his way through the abdominal contents declaring damage to virtually every organ except for the right kidney which was unscathed, and the heart surprisingly untouched. The most serious puncture wound in the grand scheme of things was that the femoral artery had been nicked in the middle of the groin.

Rowlands came to the conclusion that the young man had died of a catastrophic bleed attributed almost equally to the main organs of the body being fatally damaged, causing both a cardiac arrest which would also be the result of hypoxia due to an open and air sucking chest wound.

Huws tried his best to understand these terms and descriptions.

"I'm not convinced that he would actually have managed to walk very far at all with those injuries, whatever happened to him would have happened literally minutes before he was found. Regardless of the bleeding, the damage to his lung would have overcome him fairly quickly. He had, I suspect, a deviated mediastinum, though that's not so easy to define now post-death. This would have caused him to suffer increasing hypoxia due to pressure which in return caused a decrease in venous return and in this case, likely a rapidly reducing cardiac output. This is what will have caused the eventual cardiac arrest, though that was also the inevitable conclusion with the serious blood loss."

Most of this was way beyond Huws's level of medical knowledge. He merely nodded sagely, but recognized the extent of the atrocity that had been bestowed upon the young man.

Jane had painstakingly weighed and recorded each of the organ's individual statistics; Rowlands had inserted a flexible wire as carefully as he could through the punctures, to measure the depth of each stab wound. Indeed, as suspected, two frontal prong punctures had come through to the young man's back.

Each discovery was noted onto the voice recorder and would later be typed into the computer for final analysis.

Rowlands had by now stripped off his gown and hat and removed his shoe covers before moving through to his office with a nod of towards Huws, who was by now starving hungry. He had noticed a couple of times now this odd effect, where attending an autopsy made him feel ravenous. Strange, and not a little bit macabre.

"What do you reckon we have then?" asked Huws as they both sat down. As per usual, a small tot of whisky in their hands, their secret.

"Well," Rowlands looked down at his glass and swirled the Golden liquid around the edge of the glass. "Obviously a frenzied attack, and in my humble opinion the perpetrator fully intended to kill, I'm absolutely sure of that. The weapon of choice is your best clue here I should think, something definite to be working towards, though I imagine you are going to upset a few farming types going through their collection of old implements.

All the stab wounds have been created with the curve of the prongs pointing down, possibly in an effort also to push the victim to the ground. The horrific part of it, that had the prongs been upwards and at those depths, likely a strong-armed perpetrator would almost be lifting his victim up clear of the ground. Considerable effort would have had to be made at those depths, particularly the front to back one, to actually forcibly pull the prongs out."

Rowlands took a mouthful of whisky and promptly refilled his own tumbler.

"Doesn't bear thinking about does it?"

Huws blew out his cheeks in a long breath, and shook his head.

"We certainly have our work cut out with this case. Poor sod, what had he supposedly done to deserve such an ending? Have you ever heard of anything like this in your field of expertise?"

"No, not that I've ever heard of. I'm not aware of any journal articles published on such a thing, though I'll do a search this evening.

A pitchfork, which I have absolutely no doubt is our weapon is not usually the weapon of anyone's choice is it? A clumsy long-handled instrument. I would say that going by the victim's height of a good six-foot-two, we are looking at a likely mid-height person who has likely held the weapon angled down with both hands. I can't say whether it was right-handed or left until we find the tool and forensics do some fingerprinting analysis on it.

Our killer wouldn't need to be all that strong either, as the first stabbing, which I strongly suspect was from behind without warning, would have caused the victim to turn quickly, possibly already slightly incapacitated by the first wound, maybe even losing balance slightly, literally and metaphorically putting himself on the back foot when he turned to face his assailant. That though we will never know, it's all guesswork at the moment. I'd question why the attacker allowed him to even get away alive, that in itself was quite a risk."

Huws stood up to go. Jane had appeared in the room as Huws passed his still full glass of Laphroaig whisky back to Rowlands.

"I better not today, I need to go straight back to work, but I will gladly share a glass or two with you when we crack this case. Can you send me the report when you have completed it? And Jane, I know you will get the photos sent over? Thank you both."

Jane winked her approval of his refusal of the whisky as he said his goodbyes.

Huws was straight to the WRVS shop for a sandwich before making his way back to Llangefni, a Grab bag of crisps thrown in for good measure. Jane would not have been so chuffed at this.

Chapter Seven

THE INCIDENT ROOM was slowly taking shape again, not a room that was used on regular simple operations. It was beginning to emerge out of its mothballed normality. The place a hive of CID officers, sad at the death of a young man but excited at the prospect of something to get their teeth into again. Griff Edwards, now Detective Constable Edwards having gained his promotion at the end of last year after his exemplary efforts during the Littleton case, was in the midst of them all.

Pc Rogers, currently for some reason the only female on the team, no doubt waiting her turn to move up the promotion ladder was to Edwards' left and DS Justin Howard, to his right, head in his computer, tapping away at the keys with more skill and dexterity than Huws could ever hope to achieve.

"Right team," started Huws, chairs turning on their bases in unison to face him- except for Howard. He talked the team through what they knew so far.

Rogers leaped out of her seat towards a whirring printer, suddenly coming to life and spewing out paper after paper. Rogers picked them up and attempted to maintain their numerical order. She paused to look with more detail.

"God, who on earth would have been capable of doing such a thing around here? This is sick." She handed the first bundle to Griff Edwards, who immediately started sticking them onto the photo screen on the main wall. Noticeably he was not as keen as Rogers to see the horrendous detail.

Rogers passed him the last few and sat back at her desk.

Huws had paused until the last photograph- a head and shoulder print of the young man had been put in the very centre. Jane from the autopsy room, clearly having used her computer skills to make the young man appear open eyed and alive.

The word 'Simon' followed by a question mark written clearly on the base of the photograph. This was the only and indeed final word uttered by the young man as he died.

"OK, we have the photos and the full autopsy report will be available soon. There's little forensic evidence available from the scene as it was clearly contaminated by all involved helping on the night. The search teams are making good progress but as yet nothing much has been found. Unfortunately, the village common is intersected by many paths and is quite heavily used locally by walkers and dog owners. Horse riders as well at times. They will carry on until they have exhausted the immediate area, then our investigation will have to move further afield. Does anyone here have any suggestions at the moment before I make some of my own?"

Huws had always been one to give his team a feeling they were included in any decision-making. He believed that it made them feel part of the investigation and able to make worthwhile contributions. Sometimes they had more common sense than he gave them credit for. He himself had made his way up the ranks with the old-style policing, the hierarchy of ranks ruling with a rod of iron, discouraging any individuality, often squashing the enthusiasm for the job out of many young officers, some of who left the force for, in their own view, a more rewarding career.

Lots of decent officers had been lost this way.

Thankfully Huws had taken this on board and had always made

a conscious effort to be easier on his team. Surprisingly he still got their respect.

"Well, we need to find out who this young man is for starters," offered Rogers.

"Shall I start a social media campaign on our page Sir? I know people will no doubt guess that the person has passed away because we don't know his name. It's worth a try using the main photograph. Do you think he could maybe have been dumped out of a car?"

"Maybe, I'm sure that possibility will be investigated over the next few days. My only hesitation with a social media release is that some poor family somewhere are going to get the shock of their lives, but saying that I can't think of another option.

I wonder could we maybe just do a quick search first on the missing persons' national database, and the fingerprint database. None of the onlookers or indeed the helpers on the night mentioned recognising him, so I would assume he's not local. You know Anglesey, what do they say? It's the country's biggest village, no matter where you live in Anglesey, people seem to know everyone. Edwards and Rogers you get on with that, go ahead and coordinate the team to help you.

Howard are you working on something?"

He asked this having noticed that up to this point Howard had not even raised his head from his screen.

"Uhm, yes Sir." Clearing his throat and gulping down a mouthful out of his water bottle.

"I've just been doing a search locally to see just how many farms we have. I reckon we have at least 12 sizeable farms in the area working towards Penmon point. Most of those are still proper working farms, and innumerable smallholdings.

I've checked local hardware stores and farm shops as to whether they still actually sell pitchforks, seems they do, not that many now granted. I knew before I looked that Evans's in Borth would sell them, I've never found something they don't yet."

A slight laugh rippled through the room at this comment. Evans shop was well-known locally, they had everything a person could ever request.

Howard continued. "I thought we might just ruffle less feathers if we maybe had a sort of pitchfork amnesty as opposed to raiding all the farms and winding people up. I'm quite confident that the average farmer around here is not a pitchfork murderer.

Police forces around the country, regularly have knife amnesties where people are encouraged to bring in their knives. Maybe we could encourage local farmers and anyone else to bring in their tools. Maybe even the pub landlord would allow us to place an officer in the car park so it doesn't inconvenience people too much, we could have a collection point there. We could just label the forks with the individual owner's names for future reference as they hand them in.

According to forensics, with the force used, no matter how many times someone tried to clean the prongs there would no doubt still be traces of blood to be found. They can use Luminol which gives a glow when a light is shone on it, it reacts to haemoglobin in blood, it picks up iron, although I'm not sure if the fact these pitchforks are metal will make a difference."

Howard was directing the Luminol aspect more towards some of the less-experienced officers in the room.

"Anyway, I would assume that all the farmers who are not murderers will be totally happy to eliminate themselves from the inquiry, then the only ones we need to do a door-to-door on will be people who may own one but haven't come forwards.

This will take far fewer man-hours than having officers visit every farm and go through every antique tool that a farmer might own."

"Good work, all of you." said Huws with an appreciative nod of the head.

"If you can get that organized please Howard, just grab someone to help you. I am going to swing by to touch base with the search teams in the village, the POLSAR coordinator may have a few suggestions up his sleeve as to where he wants to put his police teams and volunteers in next, but I expect this is like finding a needle in a haystack."

"Pitchfork in a haystack Sir," said a little voice from the back of the room. Huws laughed, glad to have a little lightness amongst all the seriousness of a murder case.

"Indeed."

Huws went through into his glass-walled office to grab his coat, noticing that virtually the whole room other than Griff were now standing, looking at the detail in the photos, Griff clearly happier with the background investigations and less enamoured with the gory details.

Chapter Eight

HUWS INTENDED to drive by and have a chat with the team leader, they were perfectly capable of organizing their own work without him hovering around uselessly. The incident room team would be happy for a few hours, and he was looking forwards to a quiet relaxing evening with his feet up and some good food.

Jane had sent him a text as he was getting into his car. Well actually it was sent an hour ago but the phone signal in the county town was atrocious. He had responded quickly, hoping she hadn't thought him rude.

It would be only a short drive from the village common to Jane's house on the Glyn Garth stretch of road from Beaumaris.

He had a while ago now agreed to allow his mum to take Ben the family dog with her for company when she had eventually returned to her own home. He missed his old friend, but they had fully embraced the fact, that with his workload, and the fact that Elin his daughter was now on her first year at Aberystwyth University, living the student life as far as Covid allowed, the old dog would get more attention from his mother, as well as giving her a reason to get out of the house. She, like a lot of people, had become a little insular and fearful of going out since Lockdowns.

There was nothing happening on the search that he was needed for, a fair-sized bag of rubbish had been collected in the name of evidence, that one single shoe, that you always see on the side of a road. Huws had always wondered how someone could lose one shoe, did people just toss them out of car windows? Had they stepped in dog muck and just thrown the offending shoe away? It would always remain a mystery to him.

Other bits of clothing had been found, more than likely an item of apparel blown off a nearby washing line. There were empty cigarette boxes, plastic bottles, takeaway discards.

Huws imagined that the search teams had unintentionally done a good job of cleaning up the environment. Collateral advantage made a change from collateral damage in his book.

Gwen always got upset when people discarded their rubbish in nature. He corrected his thoughts, he still thought of her as being in the present. It still took him by surprise to remember she was not; it was always the little things that did it.

Back to the business at hand, no obvious tracks had been found up to now.

Likely a madman with a pitchfork would have stuck to existing paths as opposed to working their way through a mixture of in places knee-high dead heather, and brambles.

There was no obvious area that could be pinpointed as the scene of the attack, but it could be the young man's clothing would have absorbed an initial spill of blood until the bleeding became overwhelming. More, therefore, was evident at the location where he had finally collapsed.

Must have been a horrible way to go, thought Huws, his mind flashing back to the dreadful scene the previous year when Littleton had shot and mortally wounded young PC Steffan Parry. The scene would still on occasion play out like a film in his nightmares, always in glorious technicolour, now usurping the nightmare visions that had been a constant after the sudden death of his wife. He still at times woke up lathered in sweat, necessitating a shower in the early hours, not only to wash away the sweat but to calm him down.

Huws left them to it, only serving to waste their time with chatter. They knew to report important finds to Llangefni immediately but it appeared that the search taking many man-hours yet was unlikely to glean anything of any use.

Driving out of Allt Goch towards the busy town of Beaumaris, the hills in the distance on the mainland still had a cape of remaining winter snow. He knew from experience that they would likely still have their white hats on into the month of May, however, their outline was clear to see today, maybe bringing a slight hint that better weather was indeed on its way. The promise of a decent Easter maybe.

Dropping down the long street into the centre of the little town, it was still quiet, the tourist season as yet slow to wake up. Mainly locals, getting on with their daily business of butcher, baker, and the traditional candlestick maker errands.

Leaving the town, he saw that the first couple of yachts had been moved off the shore at the boat yard and onto their moorings. A lovely sight, considering that most had not left the yard at all during the height of the pandemic. It was a lovely little town, who could ever imagine there was a manhunt just a few miles up the road?

Eventually, he pulled off the road directly in front of the garage that came with Jane's flat. The same garage outside which Littleton had car-jacked her the previous year. He had admired her tenacity and bravery during the incident. He locked his door, stepped through the wooden door in the head height wall which would take him downhill to the cliff-hugging, glass-fronted house that was totally hidden from the road.

The wide vista of the Menai Strait stretching right and left. Bangor pier almost directly opposite. Jane had been left the property by her late mother who had lived in the house since the fifties and indeed it was still exactly as it was in her day. Nothing changed, old but stylish furniture, now considered Scandi or Vintage and probably worth more than it had been when originally purchased. Huws quite liked the simplicity and the choice of bright colours in the rugs and cushions. It felt fresh and comfortable.

Jane opened the door having already seen him come down the short path through the CCTV camera viewer.

Huws leant forward for a peck on the cheek, as he removed his coat, hanging it on the tall hall-stand. A quick glance in the wall mirror reminded him of one of his reasons to visit that afternoon, a hair-cut. Jane did a mean haircut with her dog clippers and a number three guard! He had been full of trepidation at her suggestion at first, but he needn't have worried.

A chair was waiting for him in the middle of the kitchen floor, no doubt the best barber shop view he would ever get. She draped a towel over his shoulders and started on her task. Taking as much care and precision in the smooth strokes as she would do in her autopsy work it seemed. Dark black locks fell to the ground around him.

"A perk of knowing you?" said Idris Huws with a chuckle.

"Well, if you get increasingly busy now with this case, you may be living and working out of your office again, and I don't want to be associated with a total scruff." She laughed in response.

"Fair comment." He smiled at this, knowing full well that he had seriously let himself go in the year following Gwen's death. Someone certainly needed to take him in hand and sort him out.

Haircut completed, he sat reading the daily paper, digesting the general news of the area, a quick glance at the births, marriages and deaths, whilst Jane got on with the task of making the tea.

Huws thought to himself that they were behaving like an old married couple already, comfort, feet up, telly, mutual day off walks which were few and far between, holding hands, but up to now without the so called 'benefits'. That bridge had not been crossed yet. Both currently happy for the situation to play out naturally taking its time. In fact, neither had really mentioned the issue, both happy with a cuddle.

Chapter Nine

DS JUSTIN HOWARD had taken himself up to the pub in the village of Allt Goch, though it hadn't been a quick jaunt to the local by any means. Four by fours, tractors, quads, battered, questioningly roadworthy cars all parked at random

where they had stopped, along the road near the junction outside the pub. The PC that had been given the task of collecting the pitchforks having sent out a message for assistance. Consequently, he had not as yet accepted any tools that were offered to him.

Each tool needed recording as to its ownership, name and address. Most tools clearly not having seen the light of day for decades, as was obvious by the rust and cobwebs that adorned them alongside their infestations of woodworm, going by the holes on the handles.

All the owners had agreed to grip the end of the pole which was then carefully inserted into an evidence bag and taped for security. The pronged end was also bagged and a label with the details cable tied to the middle. This would allow the forensic teams to do detailed tests on the ironwork, anything found would then mean that they had the owners details and indeed their fingerprints.

They were a motley crew of people, all no doubt discussing the incident and who may have been responsible. Indeed, was the killer amongst them right now? Surely not? Gossip would no doubt be rife in the locality.

Some of the men declared that the pitchforks would not have been used since the farming days of their descendants, hoisting a hay bale onto a trailer, two men to each bale, swinging back and up with a skill honed by years of practice.

Such was the change in farming now, no emptying of trailers at the mouth of a hay barn with a once a year used elevator taking the bales into the summer heated roof of a corrugated tin Dutch hay barn where sweat soaked men stacked the bales skilfully, all hoping that the hay had been left long enough to sun dry lest any remaining moisture created a heat great enough to ignite an inferno where the crop would combust, melting and twisting the structure of the barn itself in its ferocity.

Now it was all big bales and telehandlers. The average farmer now not actually handling a single bale from cutting to stacking. Times had very much changed hence all these men, and indeed some female farmers had gone through their outbuildings looking for these long-unused tools. Howard believed in fact that some could well be regarded as antiques by now.

The farmers all seemed quite happy to bring the tools, proof that they weren't killers. They had been asked not to wash the tools. Howard believed that the perpetrator would unlikely be amongst the farmers here today.

They took a fair bit of persuading to leave after they had left their details, enjoying the chance of a catch up.

There had been no shows at all during 2020, no Eisteddfod or Noson Lawen which were very much in the blood of these mainly Welshmen. They relished the chance to socialise, in fact it is what kept some of them sane, working morning noon and night every day of the year, some of them not seeing anyone from week to week. Company had been sorely missed.

A few had explicitly requested that they could have their tools back after the investigation, as they had belonged to long gone members of their families and had always hung in the shed where they had left them after they had last used them.

The young policeman had commented to Howard that some of them had a particular odour about them and being farming stock himself, he recognized Eau de bovine and Eau de porcine from miles away. Thankfully the majority were not like this.

Justin Howard was more concerned as to where the forensic lab would keep such a large number of potential murder weapons while they checked them over.

Howard realised by now that the Policeman with some assistance from him had got into a pattern of packing and taping and labelling. Michael the landlord was helping him to place them in the back of the riot wagon which the second officer had arrived in, being the only vehicle at the station long enough to carry the tools.

Howard left, choosing not to go straight back to the station, he drove east out of the village, past the scene of the incident which had now been opened. He followed the country lane, meandering towards the easternmost point of the island. Parking up in a wide enough spot he made his way to the end of the lane and through the gate past a solitary old Welsh cottage. Just past its front was the spot where his partner had been so cruelly gunned down. He doubted very much that the family who were sitting in the garden huddled against the spring chill had any idea of the horror that had unfolded there right in front of their garden fence a relatively short time ago.

Howard barely hesitated at the spot, choosing to continue across the open field which very gently sloped down until it reached the cliff edge above the sea. The breeze was strong, he looked out to sea, a few tankers anchored, all with their different cargoes, no doubt waiting for a pilot from Amlwch to guide them to the Mersey docks to disgorge their wares.

To his left in the distance he could see the village of Benllech, or at least a hillside full of white static caravans. No doubt the holiday makers would be back that coming summer, slightly further away was Moelfre, a quieter more peaceful beachside village, the home of one of the local Lifeboats.

To his right he could just see Ynys Seiriol or Puffin Island as a lot of people knew it, particularly the tourists. To him another location where he had dealt with a washed-up body the previous year. Who would ever imagine that for him such a beautiful place could also be the location of nightmares?

He was pleased he had his work to occupy him, but there were occasions here when he had seriously thought that it would be so easy to just disappear over the edge and be done with it. Life without Steffan just wasn't the same. All their hopes and dreams were shattered in a millisecond by a scumbag that was Littleton, a dreg of society. It would be so easy to not go on.

What kept him here? The sheer determination that he could eventually pin the murders of four people onto Littleton and not just Steff's murder. He was confident that somehow, sometime he would catch him out. He had also seen the destruction that happened within families when relatives chose to take that way out and would not want to inflict that on his friends and family. He supposed, that in itself told him it was not an option he would take. He sympathized with people who had become so tormented that they saw it indeed as the only way out. It was terrible.

Apart from anything else, DI Huws had taken it upon himself to keep a fatherly eye on him even if it was in a very subtle way that no one else noticed.

He turned his jacket collar up against the strengthening breeze and turned for his car. He had a couple of days work now, no doubt about it, matching pitchforks to his address database to tick off the bringers of tools against the ones which had as yet not taken up the opportunity, and from them he expected a good excuse, although he did recognize that it was likely that such tools may have been scrapped many moons ago in most instances.

Chapter Ten

YOUNG PC ROGERS had been diligently working on a press release that was going out the next day relating to the victim- Simon. It had been a hard poster to word but eventually she had decided on wording it in such a way that it did not imply that the pictured person was in fact already dead.

ANY INFORMATION WOULD BE APPRECIATED ON THE

CURRENT WHEREABOUTS OF THE INDIVIDUAL PICTURED.

IT IS BELIEVED THAT HE GOES BY THE NAME SIMON.

LAST SEEN IN THE AREA SURROUNDING THE TOWN OF

BEAUMARIS .

If you have any information please contact

088563002593

She would just OK this press release with DI Huws when he made an appearance, and she would be good to go on social media; the best platform these days and most likely to get a result if anyone indeed knew their man.

Putting it out there would mean that the post would be shared, via the police Facebook and Twitter pages and get to the right people.

Di Idris Huws rolled in, stripping himself of his jacket and throwing it across the spare chair in his office. Rogers was pleased to have noticed that her boss was slightly chirpier these days and the dark cloud of grief appeared to be lifting off him. He was also sporting a fairly fashionable haircut, at least for him. Jane clearly had talents in other areas apart from autopsies .

He had been terrible to deal with during the aftermath of his wife's death, the whole team knowing he had returned to work too soon, but the older members of the team had understood exactly why he chose to occupy himself.

Sadly, her team colleague Justin was going through the exact same thing and she was finding it increasingly difficult to get through to him, such was the extent that he was closing people out and entering his own little world of work. She knew it was all targeted at putting Littleton behind bars for the rest of his life.

She feared though that it was preventing him from existing in the here and now. They had all tried to get into his head, offers of meals in their respective homes all excused by, "Sorry I'm tired." or "We better not because of Covid regulations, it wouldn't be seemly to be seen breaking rules." This latter reasoning in her book, totally stupid considering they shared the same office, albeit all wearing masks.

It had got to the point where he had pushed everyone away, and beyond being civil and doing his current work he kept to himself. It was tragic to see a young DS who less than a year ago was enthusiastic and keen, now just existing day to day. His previously strong features now gaunt and eyes black-ringed from working deep into the night on any slight chance of evidence. They were all worried about him.

Rogers feared the worse when he was even a couple of minutes late to sit at his desk. He had always previously been, if anything, early to arrive. Not any more, she frequently worried that he had done something stupid to himself.

Not a 'Morning' would leave his lips, occasionally, a cursory nod of the head, but as he rarely made eye contact even that was difficult. She was hopeful that with their support he'd eventually see himself through. She herself, had other than her grandmother not lost anyone close to her. She realised that to lose your partner must be totally off the scale heart-breaking and sincerely hoped his heart would mend one day. She knew by now not to take his rejections personally but her heart broke for him.

She pushed back her chair noisily and, having noted that her DI had sat at his desk, strode across and knocked at the door of his 'glass box' as he called it. The door was always open but it was a courtesy they all gave him out of respect for his rank.

"Come in Rogers, what do you have for me? Anything I can put in front of our DCI to keep him happy?"

"Sir, I've got a press release ready to put out as quickly as we can, preferably before word spreads via gossip. We've already had a couple of journalists on the phone this morning with their speculating and predictions, even one joking about a big cat with a pitchfork.

I wanted you to OK it and I can get it out there to see if anyone recognizes this Simon. We haven't as yet declared that he was dead before he even arrived in hospital, just out of respect for any relatives who may be out there."

"Good work, as always." Responded Huws as he gave but a cursory glance over the printed sheet of paper, he knew by now that young Rogers would have done her job well.

"Go ahead, I expect with modern technology and social media we will have hopefully some sort of response today or at the latest tomorrow."

"Thank you, Sir. I'll post it now." Rogers made to leave. Huws already checking his mail inbox. To his shame, it was about the limit of his technological skills.

His phone rang and he covered the mouthpiece whilst simultaneously calling Rogers back. She turned to see him gesticulating at her to come back in whilst returning to his call. He replaced the receiver, immediately standing to respond to the information.

"Right, a rucksack has been found by the search team, they were about to close the search on that particular area, but one of the Coastguard team found it whilst he was returning to their vehicle base. He had continued the search retracing his steps which no doubt gives a different perspective and saw the bag at the base of a wall near a gate, the forensics team are making their way to the location now. Luckily the Coastguard are up on this sort of stuff now and the finder didn't interfere with it but taped the area off. The only person who will have touched it will either be the victim or the killer. If of course it turns out to be our young man's bag."

Huws was already grabbing his jacket as he was telling her the news.

"Please tell the rest of the team the latest, I'll get myself over to Forensics, so we can find out for ourselves as quickly as possible if it belongs to our victim. Get that press release out pronto."

Huws was out of the main office door in a flash. There was no time to waste when there was a person out there somewhere who could do such a thing.

Rogers, returned the press release onto her desk, then turning to face the rest of the team, she informed them of a possible development.

"Maybe it is nothing to do with our victim." Piped up a voice from the back.

"Could be someone just stopped to eat their lunch and actually walked away forgetting their bag." The same voice added.

"Well, it may prove to be the case, but they can no doubt look for any prints on it, this Simon's prints didn't match anyone in the National Database, we were told that this morning, but clearly any prints found can be matched to his now." Rogers responded with a degree of authority as the bringer of the news from Huws.

She noticed that Justin Howard who had only just arrived at the office a short while back, had barely lifted his head in acknowledgment at this small but possibly important discovery.

Returning to her desk, she clicked on the file name for the press release, had a quick look again; the public could be brutal in their criticism if there was a typo. She saved the poster in a format that would allow her in seconds to upload it onto their North Wales Police Facebook page. It would then be out there for all and sundry to see. There would be clear instructions there for anyone with any knowledge of Simon to contact them via the messenger facility, they had no time to follow the post all day, and they had very much learned that the police bashers would as always have a field day with their bad taste jokes and criticisms. Time would tell on that score. She connected the poster to the post and published it.

Within minutes, she had done exactly the same with the police Twitter account.

She would now wait the long wait to see what happened by the time it had been shared on both platforms.

Chapter Eleven

DI HUWS, pulled in to the staff car park of the Forensics Unit Suite just as a uniformed officer arrived with the discovered rucksack in an evidence bag. He was itching to grab the bag and have a look at it.

He knew it would not have been opened at the scene, whereas if one of his team had been there, no doubt they would have had a look.

Very few Bangor City residents would know that the Forensics unit was there at all, tucked discretely as it was behind a group of buildings with dull facades that belonged to the university. The staff here covered investigations that took place through the whole of North Wales, down as far as Aberystwyth in the West and Welshpool in the East of the country. He, amongst others, had fought tooth and nail to keep the Forensics provision here when Police cuts a few years ago wanted it closed and the main forensics base transferred to the Birmingham Unit. He knew full well that if this had happened cases from his area and to the East of him would be put in the back of the queue compared to the countless numbers of serious crimes that went through the Birmingham facility.

Consequently, there were only three full-time staff here, who filled their non-crime-based work with work for a very active Archaeology department that was based in the University. The Police did also on occasion delve into cold cases, however, despite what many authors may want people to believe in novels, cold cases, particularly in North Wales, were few and far between.

Huws stepped up to the glass door, pushing the speaker button on the right. He had taken the evidence bag from the officer to hand over himself.

A robotic sounding voice came from the speaker, demanding a name and reason for his presence. Seemingly satisfied, the door release bleeped.

Huws had a preference for the Forensics department compared to the Mortuary; fewer bodies, but the staff were not nearly as welcoming or forthcoming with information as his old friend Emyr Rowlands.

He made his way through to the main department, forensic technology way beyond his comprehension dotted around the brightly lit room. He cleared his throat, hoping that someone would appear to take the bag off him. His zeal to get into the bag was almost palpable.

A female staff member appeared from behind a microscope on the furthest desk away from him in the corner, approaching Huws, she asked if this was the package they had been notified of a little earlier.

"It's not contaminated is it?" she asked with some sternness in her tone, school-marmish, was the description immediately bestowed upon her by Huws.

"Of course not. We know better than to do that." He handed over the package and followed her towards her desk. She seemed a little miffed at this intrusion into her work.

"I presume you have the fingerprint records of the victim, sent to you by Jane from the autopsy suite?" he asked.

"Yes, of course we do," she snapped.

"I would like to know today, as soon as possible in fact if we have a fingerprint match, or whether there are other prints. Also, obviously, any ID that may be inside the bag, so we have more detail on this Simon." Huws spoke quietly in an attempt not to annoy this woman any more than he had apparently already done.

"We will do our best, though there are only two of us here today." She was a little brusque and dismissive.

"It's urgent. We have a press release going out as we speak asking if anyone knows our victim. It would be very useful to have some loose ends to tie up as quickly as possible. Did someone bring the pitchforks in, that were collected in the amnesty yesterday?"

Huws tried to maintain a degree of friendliness in his tone, hoping he could melt her officiousness to a degree.

"Hah yes, thanks for that- not."

She responded with more venom than Huws had anticipated.

"We'll likely will be a couple of days getting prints off all thirty-two of them and logging them all on the computer." Emphasis very much on the thirty-two.

"Hmm, there may be more to do. My young DS is currently working through his database to see which farms and smallholdings and garden centres and so on haven't handed them in. We'll need to chase those up too, though quite likely they won't all have them."

The look on her face could have frozen Llyn Padarn to its cavernous murky black depths.

Huws smiled to himself. He had met her many times over the years and the team's nickname for her of 'Miss Frosty Knickers' still seemed appropriate. He did know however that she would do a very thorough job of the task at hand. No one as far as he was aware had cracked that ice-cold exterior yet.

"We will be particularly interested to find out if, A) the rucksack belongs to our victim and B) if there are other prints on the bag at all, do they marry in with any of our pitchfork prints?"

"I will personally let you know as soon as we have that information for you." She responded this time with the teeniest flicker of a smile, just about visible in her eyes due to her mask.

Chapter Twelve

RETURNING TO THE OFFICE, DI Huws was almost accosted by Rogers in her eagerness to give him some news. She gushed in her keenness to pass it on.

The press release on their Twitter page had barely been out there for ten minutes when a response came through telling them that a member of the public had come across two lads camping in a tent at Penmon Point amongst the camper vans and motorhomes. He recognized one of them from the photo, the other being a slightly larger fellow who appeared just a tad inebriated when he met them, going by both his loud behaviour and the number of empty cans around him.

He had been parked up there for a while waiting for the tide to turn to try his hand at some fishing, and they were still there when he left in the early hours, well at least the tent was there, and he had presumed they were asleep inside it. He has since spoken to the guy at the priory pay booth, and he reckons that unless they left the point at the crack of dawn before he came to work, then they may well have headed west along the coastal path as he didn't see them.

The tent was a small two-man type in green which, Rogers paraphrased, was one of those tiny ones like a coffin. Huws knew the sort and agreed that he would suffer claustrophobia in one, let alone sharing it with another person.

"So, my next question is…" said Huws.

"Who and where is this second lad? Is he a friend? Could he be our killer? Where is the tent, because it wasn't in the rucksack found earlier? We need a plan. Get all the team into the incident room, so we can bash this out between us."

Rogers walked away to see who was in and who was out. Huws, again for the second time today, placed his folded jacket across the back of the spare chair in the office.

DS Howard popped his head around the door.

"Sir, do you have a second before you instruct the team please?"

"Of course, what have you got for me?"

"Well firstly I believe that we now are under fair pressure to declare that this is indeed a murder case, loads of people are talking about it now, and I know you wanted to find a next of kin first, but we can't leave it much longer now. Also, we have as far as I can see only a few more properties to visit relating to not handing over any pitchforks, I know some may well not have any, but if it's OK with you, I would like to take Pc Griff Edwards with me to have a look at these properties and their current inhabitants."

Justin Howard had been doing his homework and was keen to get going.

"I'm also waiting to hear whether we do have a blood result on a pitchfork from forensics too. They have a lot to get through, but with modern technology they'll soon have an idea if there are traces of blood on the points. Here's hoping."

Huws nodded his agreement and told Howard to take Edwards with him as soon as he had briefed the team but added that he wanted him to be very careful.

"Use your intuition too, whilst you are going round these places, be fully aware that it's unlikely that anyone who has willingly handed a pitchfork in is our killer, but if there is reluctance, just take care and watch your backs."

Huws was wary and watchful of Howard's emotional stability at the moment. He was tending towards being a loose cannon where his own safety was concerned. Losing Steff had changed him beyond measure. He hoped that Griff Edward's steadiness would keep things as predictable as these things could be. He was a reliable DC.

Stepping into the main incident room, there was more of a bustle. Rogers had taken another call, this time in response to the police Facebook page. How times had changed.

There used to be a time when the police had a small collection of informants who were always happy to tip them off about any wrongdoers, some in exchange for a blind eye when it came to minor discrepancies. It was not like that now. Social media had made everyone think they were law enforcement.

They all felt they knew better, and with the facelessness of being online, they were often far more critical than they would be directly. To some degree Huws tried to keep his younger officers away from it, they would be disillusioned soon enough when they realised that their main concerns were dealing with the dregs of society and not helping old ladies across roads, or with the Prosecution Services s failed to give the criminals significant custodial sentences, believing quite wrongly at times that they could be rehabilitated with help. In his experience, there was rarely enough help to make a difference. Their hands though were often tied by the higher levels of the judicial system.

Idris Huws was quietly pleased that he would be handing in his card sooner rather than later.

"There are a few people now from Facebook who saw two young men at Penmon last night. One of interest; a man who actually sat and chatted with them over a can of beer, though he didn't get their names. He said that they were both furloughed from their jobs and had decided to spend a little of their savings walking the coast of Wales from the border near Chester all the way around. They told him that they had crossed over the Menai Bridge onto the island and had walked to Penmon point the same day. Their plan was to continue anti-clockwise around the island, pitching up as close to the sea as possible, preferably without paying for spots as their funds really only allowed for food. He did comment however that the bigger lad seemed to have spent a fair bit on booze.

They planned to move on the next day, walking as far as they could, hoping to make it as far as Traeth yr Ora between Llig-wy and Dulas."

Rogers was quite pleased with her work on the press release and its response.

At least now they had an idea of the direction the young men had travelled. There was now the matter of where the second man could be, and how 'Simon' as he was known had ended up in the middle of the village of Allt Goch. Not far off the coastal path, but doubtful that he could have made it from its nearest point to where he had finally collapsed with such wounds.

Huws had listened intently to all this, never one to steam roll the enthusiasm of his team, before asking, "Right, any suggestions as to where we might go from here?"

A hand up from the back of the room.

"Can I suggest we ask the search team drone pilot to do a recce of the route of the coastal path between Penmon and Allt Goch, in case there is anyone or anything to be seen. We could ask the local Coastguard team to do a walk-through too and the lifeboat to have eyes on the cliffs from the sea?

I know that is heavily and expensively resourced but the Coast-guard will know the path like the back of their hands. I know the path quite well too but I also know that there are at least a couple of ruins on the route such as one between Caim and White Beach and another between White Beach and Bwrdd Arthur as we call it. I'm not sure if they even have openable doors, but certainly a coast-guard searcher could have a look whereas a drone might not see.

Maybe this is something we should do fairly promptly in case the second person is injured in a cleft of the cliff somewhere or maybe worse."

"Good thinking," I'll contact the POLSAR Drone Pilot, can I leave one of you to contact the Holyhead Coastguard Ops room to request a search for a potential missing person. They may well request that one of us goes there to set up a command and coordination base. I agree we need to be onto this quickly.

Rogers, did we get any sort of description of the second camper from anyone?"

"Yes Sir, a fairly good description. White Caucasian but quite tanned- looked out of a spray gun, Longish hair tied in a low ponytail, dark, virtually black. The caller reckoned around six-foot or taller, though it was difficult to be accurate as he was sitting. Quite a few days-worth of stubble. He was wearing a scruffy long-sleeved faded red top with some sort of logo on it but mainly hidden by a fleece waistcoat in black. He wore general walking black combat-type trousers and a half-decent pair of Salomon fell running-type lightweight boots."

"That was very observant of the reporter?" chimed in Howard.

"Exactly what is said," answered Rogers, "but he said that they had discussed his footwear as the man who chatted to them quite liked the look of them."

"Righto, that is a fair amount of stuff to be getting on with. Can I leave you all to be doing that, while I phone the Search Leader? Let me know if there is a problem with any aspect."

Chapter Thirteen

THE COASTGUARD TEAM'S pagers buzzed simultaneously, not all members of the local team were actually logged on for duty yet as it was still just about working day time, but the ones who were actually self-employed and able to step away from their jobs were already responding to the request messages. A flank team on either side had also been paged, to bulk up the numbers and indeed to get as many boots on the ground as possible in order to conduct a hasty search before darkness fell.

The clocks had gone forwards but on a dull day, daylight was still quick to fade into twilight.

The team were asked to rendezvous at their local station, which was within sight of the lads' last known campsite. It would have to be a search on foot, a couple starting at that point and others being dropped off at appropriate points along route. Aled, the current Station officer, was to drop team members off.

The local flank teams were already en-route to various other locations according to the radio comms,.

The teams knew they would not have a lot of light to be working with but hopefully, a sweep of the length of the route from Penmon to the east side of Llanddona beach may just be possible with the Moelfre-based team meeting them somewhere along the route.

Search bags at the ready, the comprehensive red first aid kit bag was slung over Michael's shoulders, over his life jacket. Head torch bulbs recently replenished and a hand-held fully charged torch in hand. Dyfed and Michael had the first section of the route to cover, not actually sticking strictly to the route of the coastal path initially which went slightly inland from Penmon, but instead keeping close to the clifftops past the hidden fish farm and on to the cliffs at Caim towards shore house. This was in fact an open stretch of clifftop meaning their visual capabilities were pretty good, however, if it was found that anyone had taken a tumble, they would need to get the truck to the location across the fields with the cliff rescue gear.

Both Dyfed and Michael were experienced team members, and, as the local pub landlord, Michael was party to the information regarding the victim. It had been the talk of the village over the last couple of days particularly when all the local farmers had turned up with their old and ancient pitchforks. Micheal thought it had looked like a group of tribesmen getting ready for battle, or villagers out to chase down a mythical vampire. One of the farmers had quipped that it only needed them to start singing 'Men of Harlech' for it to look like some strange version of the 1964 film Zulu. If it had not been for the seriousness of the amnesty they would no doubt have found it hilarious.

David and Ceri had been dropped off together to walk down to Shore house on the headland near the little hamlet of Caim, then continue the search towards White Beach and the high cliff headlands from that point onwards. It was fairly tough walking, deep vegetation-filled clefts having forced the coastal path away from the steep edges again, however they needed to be able to check thoroughly, so the search was not without its risks. Both Ceri and David keeping each-others backs.

They would have a couple of small clifftop abandoned buildings to check out as well on this route.

Ceri looked up as her attention was drawn to a buzz high above her head.

"Is that a drone?" she asked David.

"Yes. Police drone to do a quick recce for anything obvious. We'll be out of a job soon." Ceri chortled at this comment, "I doubt it, not until it can see under bushes and inside buildings."

"Apparently the Coastguard Service is soon to be trialling be a huge Drone alongside its helicopter search capability, then we might seriously be out of a job." responded David.

"Hah, and will it be able to splint someone's leg, stick a bandage on their head and carry a stretcher? Or do a snatch rescue in overalls and life jacket of a person in trouble on the shore?" giggled Ceri.

"Guess you're right there. Maybe we will still be useful for a while yet. They better be quick covering this stretch of coast as it will be too dark for the drone to be useful soon, or do they have night vision capability to? Now that would be-" David, didn't finish, instead he let out a grunt as he slid and lost his footing on a section of loose grit on hard soil. Thankfully he was nowhere near the edge and quickly regained his balance and composure.

"We should have bought the poles with us that we used last week on water rescue training. They would be handy to poke around in the undergrowth in front of our feet," Ceri suggested.

"Yes, I know what you mean. Feels like as waste of our time to me this though, if you were walking and carrying your camping stuff on your back, a bit like us with all this kit, would you honestly walk off a perfectly good path to walk through bracken and gorse?"

"Well, no, I wouldn't, but that's because I'm too lazy, and with being short it makes it even harder work, but if the second bloke has got into trouble out here or worse, someone has killed him too, he may well have been hidden somewhere."

Ceri was always one to have a dramatic and very overactive imagination. All her team-mates would agree with him on this. But David reckoned that this time she made good sense.

David's radio crackled, a request to give a situation report and a location. Aled would be keeping tabs on this, having just dropped Tomos and John the last two available team members at the bend in the road towards Allt Goch which would take them across the field towards the old Quarry below Bwrdd Arthur, a local ancient walled fort on a hilltop.

Hopefully, by the time they both reached the eastern edge of Llanddona beach, Moelfre team would have mustered, and although darkness was falling, the search could be repeated in reverse in a little more detail.

Dyfed and Michael had by now reached Shore House, where Ceri and David had set off, they were told by Aled via the radio to continue on their ways re-covering their team colleagues steps, until they became fatigued or alternatively, with fresh eyes, found something their team colleagues may have missed.

Searching was by no means a walk in the park, irrespective of distance, the terrain good and bad had to be covered.

They had however reported back to Aled that absolutely nothing of significance had been found other than the remains of burst helium balloons that Dyfed hated and had stuffed in his pockets and the usual collection of empty crisp packets, nothing however to indicate they were freshly dropped. Michael had in fact suggested that for the remainder of their search that maybe they should now make their way inland a hundred metres or so onto the actual coastal path which Ceri and David would not as yet have searched.

Aled's answer was in the affirmative, it would make the search slightly easier underfoot anyway. Darkness was enveloping them rapidly now. Shadows cast by wind-beaten, still winter-bare trees, creating false figures around each twist in the path. Out wintered cattle trodden earth, hiding potholes deep enough to break a grown man's leg.

"So much for being easier on the path," thought Dyfed to himself."

Tomos and John had walked across the field down towards a relatively newly flagged section of the coastal path. A landslide on an older part a few years ago had caused a track lower down the hill to crumble so it was barely wide enough for a quad, effectively cutting off two cottages from access by car.

The new path had created a diversion down to an old quarry on the shore just to the east of Llanddona beach itself, the remains of the old buildings were still there to be seen. Evidence of barbecue fires were dotted around, and something that Tomos couldn't see the point of- piles of stones, miniature cairn like structures of large pebbles topped with ever smaller ones. It seemed that nowadays human beings could not visit anywhere unless they left some mark of their presence.

John had not been down to this particular beach for a couple of years now, when they had been called to assist the police in the removal of a body off the shore. It was barely a body such was its decomposition, virtually a clean sun-bleached and salt spray weathered skeleton with no distinguishing features at all to be recognized.

It had turned out to have been a missing person who had been lost a fair while, he couldn't recollect the name, but his next of kin had been traced. At least the man had been put to rest. That was one consolation.

The two men had a good look at the shoreline and within the rusting concrete and iron hulk of the building. They then returned up the steep slope, Tomos blowing in response to the effort.

ly

"Hey, for a young lad, you are shockingly unfit", joked John. "Too many pies and pints no doubt."

"Get lost. I can still keep up with a search can't I?" snarked Tomos.

John was likely twenty years his senior, old enough to be his father, but whenever he got the opportunity, was always off up some mountain or out surfing or kayaking. He knew this coastline literally like the back of his hand, every inch of it.

"Yes, you can still search now, but will you still be able to in twenty years' time, or even ten? At the rate you are blowing we will be needing to stretcher you out."

Tomos did not reply to this comment, truth hurt, he knew he

needed to lay off the beer. Head down and no doubt sulking he continued up the slope.

"Hangfire there, before we get back to the top of the hill, let me just go to the left here. There's a huge flat area there where some of the old machine workings are. The quarry cliffs are above us again. Just in case someone has had a mishap from above."

He didn't hear Tomos's hiss of exasperation at having to retrace his steps, but he could sense the lads' reluctance even with his back to him. The slope up to the left needed careful scrambling, it crossed a gulley cut into the hill where the old incline would have taken huge blocks of granite down the hill onto the loading conveyor belt down to the waiting ships. Days long gone now, only a deep ravine remained with a few rusted iron uprights where the wooden sleeper crosspieces had long rotted away.

He could hear Tomos muttering under his breath as he scrambled hand over foot to follow, he was certainly not a mountain goat. John almost went as far as to think that he was a little, if not a big liability. Anyway, there was no time for criticism now, he hauled himself up the last section of the steep bank and straightened himself up in order to have a quick scan, it was dark by now but their torches gave good localized light. He tried to explain their bearings to his companion, lest unfamiliarity with the terrain led him too far over to the edge. There were hollowed-out, water-filled craters hereabouts that were certainly a trip hazard. John decided that they should have as close a look as they could initially on the seaward side of the quarry level then move further in under the carved away cliff above them. It was a good fifty metres or so above them to the top. Enough to kill anyone.

Rocks and boulders were strewn around and about as if a giant had tossed them down from above, each one needing a walk around for fear of anyone being on the far side in the shadow of the torch beam. They had separated slightly now, John confident to allow Tomos to widen his range slightly as they were further from the cliff edge.

He contacted Aled by radio just to give an Obs normal, as they had been directed to do on a search, every fifteen minutes or so, giving a location grid reference at the same time. So much easier now with modern apps than when he first joined and had to use large sheet maps which were never practical especially in the wind.

Suddenly Tomos gave a shout, "I think I might have found something."

John walked over to where Tomos was shining his torch at some green fragments of material that were singed at the edges. A boulder placed directly on top of it partially hiding it from anyone but the keenest of eyes. Someone didn't want it found that was obvious. The ground around it was also scorched.

"What colour was their tent?" asked Tomos. "Green" answered a subdued John.

"Well done lad, good spot in the twilight, your eyesight is obviously better than the state of your lungs."

"Aye, well, we all have our individual strengths don't we," responded Tomos, clearly a dig at his colleagues' previous criticisms.

"What do we do now?" asked Tomos, "I suppose we need to let someone know?"

"I'll radio Holyhead Ops room direct as our Sector manager will be liaising with the police as Silver Command and include Aled in the comms. Don't touch anything else there, we can tape it off in a minute, but while I radio, just have a look around in case you see anything else obvious." Aled was already finding the grid reference for the location as he took his hand-held radio unit off its clip.

"Right you are." Tomos seemed enthused, at last. So many searches ended up with nothing found, hoaxes, missing people who weren't missing, but had been discovered somewhere else, that he seemed pleased to have actually made a discovery himself. He set about having a more detailed look round with new-found vigor and enthusiasm.

John had been told to stand by for further instruction by the Ops room who had passed the message on to the police, likely they would have to stay there until the police arrived.

When eventually the directions came, Aled told John that a number of the Moelfre team were going to await the police at the corner of the lane atop the cliff to lead them down to the location, then they would radio when nearer for more definitive directions. John and Tomos were to sit it out. Likely Ceri and David would be with them soon but John was asked to keep as few people as possible near the find so as not to contaminate the area.

They may well be in for a long wait. At least it wasn't raining. Tomos took it as an opportunity to have a sit down and light a cigarette.

Chapter Fourteen

IDRIS HUWS HAD ONLY JUST SAT down in his armchair with a small tot of whisky in a glass. He'd just ended a phone conversation with Jane when it rang again just as he lifted the glass to his lips.

Returning home as the opportunity arose for a change of clothes, as his team had everything in hand regarding the search, once the police drone had completed what it could of the headlands before the light went, there wasn't an awful lot they could do until the coastguard had completed their more detailed search. He didn't envy them the task. He knew it was a hard, tough section of the Anglesey coast. No doubt it would be morning before they heard **any more**. He just hoped it would be positive.

The unexpected phone call had been made by DS Howard, who had returned late from his initial visits to the non-complying farmers. No doubt he was preparing to work late into the night. Huws also knew that as soon as he had completed his Pitchfork database as his fellow officers had named it, he would be back into his Littleton file. Huws knew better by now than to dissuade him from his repeated trawls through the evidence. He worried it would send Howard over the edge into an early grave one way or another.

"Sir, news has just come in via silver command that the Coast-guard searchers have found what may well be the remnants of the two guys' tent, we can't be sure yet, other than partly burnt material has been found partially covered by a boulder. Someone was clearly trying to hide it. It's freshly burnt not historical as the scorch marks and burnt fragments still smell fresh."

He paused as if unsure of himself.

"I hope I have done the right thing, but I've taken the liberty of sending PC Rogers and DC Edwards to the scene to secure it until we can get forensics there. The coastguard officers on scene assured Silver Command that they had not touched the tent and had taped the area off. They have a couple of team members who are going to meet our officers and take them down there. Not the easiest place to get to apparently, particularly in the dark."

Howard waited for the response from the other end of the line. A brooding lack of confidence in his own judgment emanating from the silence. He never used to be like that.

"Of course, you have made the right decision lad, exactly what I would have done. Has anyone contacted Miss Frosty Knickers yet to let her know she is needed again, and at this hour of the evening? I would not want to be the person making that call." He laughed.

"Yes Sir, already done." There was no humour in Justin Howard's response. He did not seem to see the light side of anything these days. A shadow of his former self emotionally and physically.

Justin continued.

"The coastguard on scene have also offered to get their truck to the nearest access point to the quarry level and set up their genera-tors and lights, not just to illuminate the scene forensically but just to make their access a little safer. The only other option was to wait until morning and access by helicopter. I gave the go-ahead for the lighting this evening as I didn't think we wanted to waste any time in case this second man is alive and injured somewhere."

"Great work, yes, that is all ideal, I had just settled in my slippers by a fire with a glass of warming whisky, but thankfully hadn't let it pass my lips yet, give me the location again and I will make my way down there too."

Justin Howard explained in detail where he was to go.

" So, is this roughly the same area where the remains were found a couple of years ago then when we had the incidents with that bloody cat?" asked Huws.

"Yes Sir, no more than a couple of hundred metres further east by all estimations."

"Righty ho, phone me if you hear of anything else while I am on my way there." Huws was already out of his chair, glass still in hand tucking the phone into his jacket pocket as he went to put it on. Almost without thinking he downed the whisky in one gulp, his excuse to himself was that it may well be a long night and could quite possibly get cold.

He closed the empty house door behind him and clicked the fob to open the door of his car, his new car, all the comforts, Bluetooth, electric windows, all the works, sat nav. One of his young officers had kindly set everything up for him, meaning all he needed to do was to leave the Bluetooth on his phone in the one position and his phone became hands-free. All new technology to him. He was still however saddened that his old dad's hand-me-down Ford Granada had eventually died a death, not to be resurrected. He had not been able to bring himself to get rid of it though. It now had pride of place outside his old mother's house where it had spent its younger years. His mother said it made her feel safer to have the car outside her house, however, it seemed to also have become home to various gardening paraphernalia that she had no room for in her garden shed. He imagined that knowing her, she would be growing tomatoes inside it later in the year. He chuckled to himself at that thought.

Chapter Fifteen

ROGERS AND EDWARDS had arrived at the top of the road, still a good half-mile hike across the field to the location, the gate on the corner had been opened by the Coastguard crew who had made their way down in a truck ahead of them. Rogers parked as close to the hedge as she could having already deposited Griff Edwards further down the road. She was reluctant to enter the field with a vehicle at the risk of getting herself stuck in the still damp soil of early spring. Her father a keen gardener would always say that he could smell spring in the air. It was only now as an adult that she appreciated what he meant. Griff was off ahead of her striding down the field, she was determined not to leg it after him, knowing that it would be just like her to slip and fall flat on her face, no she would maintain a modicum of decorum and walk down carefully.

A sound behind her caused her to pause then squint in the bright light coming down the field behind her.

A coastguard truck caught up with her and pulled up alongside.

"Fancy a lift?" asked a fluorescent buff masked man, well she presumed he was. Wearing his helmet, the only part of the face she could make out were the eyes.

"My name is Aled, local coastguard team member. I've no one

in the back so as long as you are happy to sit diagonally behind me and wear a mask, I will give you a lift down as close as we can get, will save your boots from getting quite wet by the time you get there."

I Aled was making his way down to join the rest of the teams on scene. Their job now would be to hang around and be of any assistance should they be able to do anything. He had all the lighting gear and the generator in the back of the crew cab truck. It would no doubt be of great help.

The graveled track leaving the field in a sharp descent to the quarry was already taped off with a young PC on duty to prevent entry, not that there were many random walkers there at this by now increasingly late hour. There was no sign of Griff thought Rogers as she alighted from the vehicle now parked adjacent to a long low building to her right.

She shone her torch towards a glassless window, just an iron grill left in the concrete frame.

"The grills in the windows were to prevent the windows being hit by bits of stone when they were blasting the quarry. These buildings were the barracks at one time. Most of the men hereabouts worked here. Limestone was quarried here I believe whereas further round past Penmon point they quarried for Granite.

The men who did not live within walking distance would have lived here during the week. They were tough hard-working men in those days." Aled was full of chatter and information.

"The workers were probably much fitter than a lot of us now I should imagine," responded Rogers.

She carried on past the buildings hot-footing it behind Aled who seemed at least to know exactly where he was going. The scramble through the gorge was not what she had planned on doing that evening. Just beyond the gorge, they caught up with Edwards who looked a tad more dishevelled than he had been ten minutes previously.

"You look a mess?" questioned Rogers.

"Uhmm, yes well, I went over my ankle in a water-filled hole then slipped on my arse trying to get out the other side."

He was clearly embarrassed whereas his colleague thought it hilarious and well-deserved for lolloping ahead like a great wazzock just to get there first. He had gained nothing other than a filthy coat and wet feet.

A couple of Coastguard officers were by now walking back to their truck to fetch the generators and lights, in no time at all the place was lit up like some spooky film set, shadows of giant long-legged people playing like a film against the backdrop of the quarry cliff to their landward side.

People in white coveralls and masks arrived, well at least two people did. Rogers and Edwards watched on as initial photographs were taken then the boulder rolled off the material revealing more of the crumpled and singed fabric. When pulled out, it was clear to see that it was indeed a tent.

Strangely enough, there were no other remnants to be seen, no clothing, no indication that anyone might have actually chosen to camp here, there were however to be found in the brightness of the lamps a clear skid mark on the wet ground, evidence something had been dragged.

There was suddenly a loud swearing, rapidly disguised by a cough from behind Rogers and Edwards, both turning towards the noise, nothing could be seen as they were glaring right into the powerful lamps, blinded. The cough took on a shape and slowly but surely, out of the silhouette came DI Huws, how the hell he had made it down there God only knew, in his hand was his mobile phone with the torch function switched on. Edwards however, although no comment was made, was quite pleased to notice that he wasn't the only one with wet feet. He allowed himself a smile behind his mask.

Within a short time, forensics had marked, photographed and packaged the evidence that they had found at the scene and were making to leave. Idris Huws strode across to have a word.

They assured him that they would start their investigations in earnest early next morning, well in fact, that morning, it was already now gone midnight. Huws thanked them for turning out then returned to face his own officers.

"How many bodies do we currently have now?" he asked Rogers who for a minuscule second just looked at him askance if not slightly alarmed.

"Oh, you mean how many officers do we have on scene?" she retorted.

"Well yes, of course, it's what I mean. I didn't mean dead bodies! We will need a couple to stay at the top of the road to stop any walkers from coming down the path. I doubt we will get much footfall this time of night but on the other hand, we do know that there are few people hereabouts who have a penchant for a few rabbits. Better safe than sorry. Rogers do you know when they came on duty?" asked Huws. No doubt thankful that he was not of the rank where he would be asked to sit in a car at the entrance to a field all night.

"I think two of them are on a ten till six shift so not long been on rota, whereas the third was on a two- ten so should have been off by now." Edwards butted in with this answer.

"OK, send the two-ten home, the other two can stay, it will be a long night for them, but no doubt preferable to dealing with drunks way past kicking out time."

Edwards made his way carefully, not wanting another embarrassing fall, to find the two unfortunate officers to deliver his bad news. However, neither was particularly bothered. One lived locally and told his colleague that he would ring his wife who would no doubt when asked bring them both a flask of hot tea and a butty.

"Really!" exclaimed his team buddy, "My wife would no doubt kill me or give me the cold shoulder for a month if I rang her this time of the night with that request."

"Well, there you are, see? I'm lucky to have such a caring wife."

"Oh, it's not that she doesn't care, it's just that if she had a call off my phone in the early hours, she would panic thinking something had happened to me, you know how they can be, I'm allowed to send her a quick text at ten-thirty which is when she would usually go to bed, to say night, but on a shift like tonight when I would have only left the house at nine-thirty, she would be worried."

While he listened to their inane banter, Edwards walked back to join on to Huws's slow crawl up the steep hill back to his car. The Coastguard team were busy packing away their lighting equipment making ready to also call it a day, waiting for the stand-down message from the Ops room. Unbeknown to them until Huws had given his own guy the information, that they were done at the scene then he in turn would not convey the stand down order through Silver Command. It could be a long night for the Coastguard team too.

Ceri had already complained that she was starving and had already found a bush behind which she had a pee, it was no easy task for a female coastguard to strip out of their one-piece overalls to bare her bum. Thankfully it was dark, but Tomos, as was usual, still laughed and shouted that he could see a new moon rising.

Chapter Sixteen

THE TWO OFFICERS who had supposedly kept watch on the field entrance that night were the butt of all jokes by morning, both caught fast asleep at six am by a passing farmhand on his way to milking duties. Heads lolled, mouths agape, all plastered on Facebook by the time DI Huws arrived at the office. He was not best pleased, well at least he appeared less than chuffed to the rest of the sniggering team, but he had always had a sense of humour, and most bobbies would be caught out in a compromising position at some point in their service. He knew damned well that there was no need for either himself or their duty sergeant to give them a roasting, the embarrassment alone would suffice. He would not mention a word. They would both have gone off duty at six anyway, or when they woke up and would no doubt have had this faux pas pointed out to them by colleagues and family.

DS Howard was keen to make use of PC Edwards again to go and finish off the few visits they had still to do of people who were yet to hand in their tools. The day had been cut short yesterday due to the search. Howard reckoned that bar any incidents they'd be finished by lunchtime. Most of the people they had visited so far were perfectly happy for the two officers to have a quick look around their barns. Some of which were no longer barns, but cleared out, renovated, and in use as pony stables, or craft rooms. They visited two potteries and a carpenter.

Where the sheds stood untouched, they had been allowed access, and other than one pitchfork that they asked to take with them, they found nothing else other than rusty old horseshoes, broken buckets, and lots of cobwebs. The lady who was happy to hand over the pitchfork was unaware it was hanging by two nails off an old manger and had no idea whatsoever what it was. Edwards had suggested to Howard that they left it shrouded in its cobwebs, clearly not having been moved for maybe decades, but Howard insisted it joined the others in the lab.

There were four properties left for today, and they planned to start with the furthest from Allt Goch and make their way towards the village, starting at the small hamlet of Glanrafon. The first second and third properties proved empty, with no one at home. Holiday cottages by the looks of things and quite likely had been empty due to Covid restrictions.

Justin Howard took a deep breath, the vivid picture of that little white holiday cottage near Penmon, that fateful day when the love of his life Steff was shot entered his head as if the thought itself was a bullet. Moments like this were very much still the source of borderline panic attacks. Something which so far had only happened in the privacy of his own home.

Thankfully he managed to compose himself. Edwards had done a brief recce of any outbuildings, but it was clear by the renovations that had taken place that the buildings would not contain any farming relics.

They drove the road towards Allt Gosh, passing the bend in the road where their colleagues had been well and truly shown up that morning. They both laughed at this recognition. A fresh traffic unit car was parked there now, the officer guarding the field entrance not showing any recognition as they drove past.

A further search was to be made by officers drafted in to assist with a more generalized daylight search of the quarry.

"I'm glad I don't have to go paddling about in the muck and

puddles down there today, my shoes still haven't dried out from last night," commented Griff.

"Well, you should have known better and taken some wellies with you for that sort of job, lesson learned hey? We just need to take a right here and the next farm is on the right down a track. We've been here before, last year. The old guy that lives there is a bit of an odd bod, do you remember? He was that Ashley Evans's father. One of the drug runners who was shot last year down at White beach. I doubt very much that we'll be made welcome." Justin was obviously not savouring the thought of meeting the old boy again.

"Ah yes, I know who you mean. Well I hope you're prepared to get filthy. From what I remember some lads, who attended last year said it was like a museum. It seems that he has never discarded a single implement or machine for years and years. There are likely tools there from his great grandparent's days, if he is third, fourth-generation owner."

Griff appeared strangely enthusiastic at the prospect.

"Why so keen?" asked Howard.

"Oh, just that you never know what gems you might find some-where like this," they had now turned down the drive, no improvement to its rough surface apparent. If anything, it had deteriorated.

"I quite like collecting old farm implements, my father and I enjoy doing them up and when we have time, we go to the odd vintage steam rally."

"Really! Wow, I would never have guessed. No wonder you were keen to come with me on this job. You learn something new about someone every day." Justin Howard laughed. Edwards was pleased to hear his old buddies humour making an appearance.

Howard added with mock seriousness, "I will have to keep a beady eye on you then, that you don't slip some old relic into the boot when I'm not looking."

"Yes, you should." It was good to laugh.

The rough track was never-ending, they could see the farmhouse up ahead nestled in a fold of the hill. The builders in those days were totally unimpressed by sea views. It was far more important to build a property where a hillock or similar protected the farm from the worst weather. In this case, the farm was enveloped on three sides by its almost roofless outbuildings. You needed to be in one of the small attic windows to even get a glimpse of the sea.

Nothing seemed to have changed since their last visit. The same big bale feeders stuffed with ancient feed sacks and orange bale string, stood next to a transport box designed to go behind a tractor that would no longer carry anything as its floor had rotted away. A long-handled four-pronged fork held a rusting corrugated shed door closed. Howard was quick to don gloves and grab the fork. A blue Fordson Major tractor stood forlornly in a corner, it's flaking red-painted wheel rims sitting on flattened tyres, greened from the rot of dried animal muck.

It was a sad picture of dereliction and despair. Howard could tell by the gleam in Edwards's eye that he could barely wait to get into some of the sheds.

First, they had to find Mr. Evans and persuade him to let them have a look around.

"I hope to God he plays ball, and that we don't have to bloody come back with a warrant, from what I remember he was not the most agreeable person to deal with before.

In fairness though that might have been due to the fact that we had come to tell him of the death of his son. I wonder if he ever took responsibility and buried him. I know there was no love lost between them, but I think if I'm right, that he was his only next of kin."

Justin tailed off his conversation as he made his way towards the door.

Before he could knock his phone rang. He paused, took his phone out of his pocket, and saw it was Huws.

"Yes Sir, what can we do for you? We are on our last but one property." he told his superior.

"How quickly can you get down to the quarry, I'm assuming you can't be that far away. They've made a bit of a discovery down there inside the remains of the old barracks building on the slope on the way down. A building we all passed on the way down there yesterday. I've already notified Forensics who are going to get there as soon as they can." Huws seemed fairly excited at this development.

"We can always come back to this place in the next day or so if we need to. We'll be no more than twenty minutes., I can basically see the quarry from the end of the drive."

"Thanks lad, young Rogers is on her way there too, she even said when we heard, that she had shone her torch at the building's windows last night as she walked past it but not thought to look in."

He repeated all this to Griff Edwards and made to leave. He could have sworn that he heard the shuffling of feet behind the wooden house door. That would not have been difficult due to the dog or rat chewed bottom edge leaving a considerable gap underneath it.

They would be back.

They drove up the track as carefully but as rapidly as they dared, out onto the single-track road, headed to the junction and a quick left, and they were at the corner where, by now a few officers had congregated, some for refreshments, others to await orders from the quarry below. On questioning, they weren't sure what the actual discovery had been, but there was blood apparently.

Chapter Seventeen

PC ROGERS ARRIVED a matter of minutes after Howard and Edwards. Clearly she had kept her foot to the board on the way from Llangefni. She was out of the car and opening the boot, fetching a pair of wellingtons as quick as a flash.

All three set off across the field, which led them through a gate onto a short section of rough gravelled path before descending through another field and on to a metal gate leading to a steep track down to the quarry. This route had not been in existence for years, but the recent diversion in the coastal path had once again made this area of coast accessible to the walking public.

The old barracks were three-quarters of the way down the slope, so Edwards was pleased to see that no mud was involved.

The building was already taped off. Justin Howard turned at the sound of feet behind him and made way for the two forensics personnel who wafted past them.

The general search of the area had continued at first light. On entering the old barracks there had been the ash remains of a campfire, a few tent pegs which seemed to have been pulled out and discarded and a considerable amount of blood spatter on the ground.

Howard placed some slip-on covers on his feet and entered the building behind Miss Frosty knickers- he had to take care not to refer to her by that name out loud. She was her usual dour self this morning, busy clearing the area and taking photos of clear footprints that could be seen marking the damp soil floor. There were two or three different sets as far as Howard could see without making a great effort to look.

"Watch where you are putting your feet." demanded her Ladyship gruffly.

"Of course." answered Howard in a falsely meek tone. He didn't want to get on the wrong side of her.

"There seems to be an awful lot of dried blood here," he commented. "Quite a smear of it, as if someone has been dragged or crawled?"

"Let's not speculate, but yes, a lot of blood, considering that a fair amount may well have been absorbed by this soil floor," she offered in response.

"Do you think this is where our Simon victim was attacked?" he asked again, fully aware that she particularly disliked being questioned while she was in the middle of an initial appraisal.

"Absolutely no way!" she retorted with some force.

"There is no way that young man could have walked across the field and into the village had he lost that amount of blood here, totally impossible. He would unlikely even have made it to the top of the slope before losing consciousness through hypovolaemia. I will quite confidently say, even before we crossmatch blood samples that this blood very likely has come from another victim who it appears has been brutally attacked. From the blood smears, I would also say with certainty that the victim was dragged and here," she pointed at the ground where the blood stopped abruptly, "I would suggest the victim may have been placed on a tarpaulin or plastic sheet and dragged away and out of the building."

She knew her stuff thought Howard. But he was dying to tell her she was speculating too.

Edwards butted in.

"Could they maybe have been dragged out somewhere on the

tent? It looks as if they may well have set up camp for the night inside the shed?"

"Anything is possible." She answered.

Rogers was busy checking her phone, she raised her head.

"We have a positive ID on the two men from the posted photo. He isn't Simon at all, he is called Christopher, or Chris Tennant. Left his home over a week ago to walk the coastal path with his mate Simon Chatterris, his close friend Paul Murdock has left us a message. He says he has not heard from either of them for a few days, and they were normally very active on Facebook, Instagram, and Twitter, posting photos of their journey. They were aiming to try to camp in as many 'Different' places as possible."

"So, our body is not Simon at all, his mate was Simon, and this person, now known as Chris, may well have been trying to warn us or tell us that something had happened to Simon. Jeez, how confusing." Edwards shook his head.

Howard added, "The question now is where the hell is Simon?" This job was getting bigger by the minute.

Chapter Eighteen

THEY LEFT the forensics team to their work; having very much been made to feel as if they were in the way. Making their way across the gorge again, Edwards as per usual complained about the terrain and the hidden water-filled holes. A shout behind them drew their attention to DI Huws making his best effort to look elegant and graceful as he clambered to join them.

On firmer ground, they paused, Rogers filled him in on the latest developments online, watching Huws shake his head as she described the Facebook message.

"Iesu Grist, is nothing ever straightforward hereabouts? it's getting like bloody Midsummer Murders on the telly now, where there won't be anyone left by the time they had solved the episode. He added that they needed to update the ground search teams with the new information so the search plan could be adapted and changed if necessary.

Howard almost smiled at the Midsummer Murders quip; he was sure his boss had used that comment before. But he conceded that he was quite right to make the observation because as far as he was aware there had been eight deaths within a short radius of the village over the last few years albeit some of them attributable to a big cat which had seemed to have gone to ground since then, or else died.

"The biggest challenge here today I think," motioned Huws with his arms, "is avoiding being shat on by these bloody seagulls, there are loads of them."

"Likely it's their breeding season, or they are ever hopeful that we will have a ready supply of sandwiches and ice cream cones for them to nick." laughed Edwards, who agreed that there seemed indeed to be an inordinate number of the flying vultures as he called them.

"Maybe there are shoals of mackerel out at sea." suggested Rogers.

"Unlikely," answered Edwards, " There is an R in the month, It's too early for them."

"Clever clogs, I wasn't aware that fish could read a calendar."

"We have just likely disturbed them." said Huws, trying to regain a modicum of seriousness in the conversation as the Police search and Rescue team chief strode across towards them, though he did think to himself that the number of birds and the deafening sound of their airborne squawking was highly distracting. He indicated the nuisance of the noise with a look to the sky and rolling of the eyes, before speaking.

"We have done a pretty thorough job now of the quarry level where the material remnants were found. Nothing much else to find. The vegetation is fairly dense in patches, and we can't find any evidence that anyone has particularly been having a party or anything else up here. There is really only one way in and out of this level." He nodded towards the rough path that they had taken through the gorge. "So, any footprints other than our own would no doubt have been destroyed since last night with all the access and egress traipsing."

Huws was not best pleased that he was almost suggesting that his officers had destroyed possible evidence.

The POLSAR officer continued.

"There is no access from the east, and a sheer drop to a lower ledge below, we can't get eyes on there without a fair bit of scrambling which I consider too dangerous. My team are not rope rescue trained. Can I suggest that we ask for the local Coastguard team to attend again? I believe they are a cliff team that used to work like this. If we can just get a couple of them over the edge to have a good look. I've worked out the tides and even at high tide in a couple of hours the ledge below will still be too high from the seaward side for the lifeboat to come alongside and have a good look."

He paused whilst Huws thought of his response. His DCI would no doubt start to ask questions again at the costs involved. But he agreed that it was probably the best way to go about it. He told the search officer he would make the call and that maybe in the meantime he should take the opportunity whilst they waited for the arrival of the Coastguard to give his team a break and get some refreshments.

Everyone agreed on this plan, quickly forming a centipede-like line of search officers making their way up the hill, followed by Huws and his entourage. Huws broke off to notify forensics of their plan. They would be a little while again, but nearly had all they needed for their tests.

On arrival back at the road Huws was pleasantly surprised to see most of the officers biting into sandwiches and various snacks.

The pub landlord Michael had kindly prepared a load of food and bought it down in his van. Huws thanked him on behalf of the teams and broke the news to him that likely in a few minutes his pager would go. Michael stated that he always had his Coastguard kit in his vehicle anyway and would change and wait for his team to arrive from their base. He was confident they would not be long. The truck would get as far as just below the barracks anyway and if they had a good team response then there would be enough of them to carry the ropes, stakes, and winch to the top of the cliff.

Huws thanked him, and made his way through the throng to make sure there was something left to eat.

Chapter Nineteen

DYFED WAS JUST PUSHING the hydraulic lift button on the car ramp when his pager went. He read the message on the screen- A cliff search job on the ledges in the old quarry down below the village of Allt Goch- missing person. A grid location was given; however, Dyfed was well aware of where the location was. Was this a continuation of yesterday's job he wondered; maybe more information had come to light?

He was bringing the ramp down with one push of the button whilst he was telling his two mechanics that he had to go. They were well-used to their boss disappearing, and he was confident that they would do a good job in his absence.

He hoped that Aled and Michael were available as well, being cliff tecs. John's presence would be handy too. Ceri and Tomos may well not be logged on today, being employed they did not have quite the freedom to respond as he had.

He was in his car and on the way to the Coastguard station, to fetch the truck, likely John would be there to meet him. Being local to the location though he hoped that Aled and Michael would already be en route to the rendezvous point.

This part of the cliff was not totally familiar to them, but no doubt now that it was accessible to the public, it would become a more common feature in their territory as more walkers discovered it.

His VHF radio was on and on the passenger seat, he heard the flank team at Moelfre being paged, clearly there had not been enough response to fully service a cliff team with just their station. He was, sure as always, that a good job would be carried out.

The road down to the station was reasonably quiet thankfully, the summer holidays were not quite so straightforward. Many visitors he reckoned only able to reverse a short distance around a street corner as per the UK driving test whereas going back a hundred yards or so to a passing place was beyond some and wasted considerable time for them. He opened the garage roller door and jumped in the truck, got out to close the door, and with there being no sign of John he set off towards the call-out location near Allt Goch. If he saw him on the way, John could dump his car and jump in.

Michael was already in his coveralls and helmet when Aled arrived. They both set off together down the hill. They could at least evaluate the best spot to set up the gear whilst they waited for whomever else may turn up.

Dyfed had already called them via their call sign to tell them he was en route. Three would be the bare minimum realistically to do a descent but more volunteers would just make the task easier.

There was no need for any panic and blue lights on the road towards Allt Goch, the road was clear until he got to the corner in the road where all the police vehicles had parked, he could barely squeeze through, but he was waved on down through the gate and into the field. He had met DI Huws previously and slowed down to a stop alongside him. He was filled in on the task ahead of them and informed that his colleagues had already set off down.

"Ah, and here arrives another Coastguard truck behind you," said Huws.

The second truck pulled up next to Dyfed, the adjoining team's station officer who was the passenger hopped out.

"What's the score?" he asked.

Dyfed filled him in, they were to drive the vehicles down as far as possible. Dyfed's truck had all the necessary cliff gear on board, but extra hands would be really useful to carry the equipment to the clifftop. He explained that two of his team members had gone ahead but clearly the availability was a little thin on the ground.

There were two volunteers in the second truck, but they had been assured that two more team members were en route in their own vehicles and would obviously make their way down on foot.

Whilst making their way downhill to the quarry Dyfed imagined that the farmer whose land they were traversing would not be best pleased with the tyre tracks in the still damp grass sward. That however would recover given time.

Arriving at the only piece of flat land just beyond the barracks where a flat splay had been created at some time. Dyfed looked across to his right and saw both Michael and Aled making their way across the gorge towards them.

"Many hands make light work and all that, we should be able to take what we need in one trip across to where we think best for the stakes. Two of us can take the winch, between us. The rest of you can bring the rope bags and stakes. Don't forget the quadpod or maybe leave that for the other two to bring when they get there."

Dyfed was just pulling bags out of the back of the truck, hands grabbing what was needed. They set off carefully to the chosen spot.

Aled had imagined that getting stakes in was going to be a fair challenge and there was certainly nothing else up there that would be a secure belay. He would soon be proved correct. It was taking some pretty persuasive sledge hammering to secure a strong safe stake hold.

All the kit was laid out on the bright orange dump sheet, carabiniers linked like home-made paper Christmas decorations. Various pulleys and gadgetry, all familiar within this well-trained group.

Dyfed gave the winch a quick pull, confident it wouldn't let them down, a confidence from built from continued maintenance and regular checks. Two volunteers were already donning cliff harnesses as the other team members arrived carrying the necessary quadpod which would be placed on the edge of the cliff. The stakes would be used to secure the two clifftop operators to enable them to safely place the quadpod and edge protector sheet on the very edge of the clifftop lest the ropes be scuffed on the sharp rock edge.

Michael was donning a third cliff harness and setting himself up with the equipment needed to send himself over the edge under the observation of the cliff top personnel.

Aled checked over Michael's equipment before he attached himself onto the main rope and safety line which were rigged to the top to allow him a safe descent. He passed himself through the quadpod, a colleague secured on each side to their own stakes. Michael was a tall man, so his ducking under the top of the metal setup was less than elegant. A last radio check between him and Aled, who remined ready to man the ropes, and he was ready to step backward off the cliff. Not something that appealed to everybody.

Indeed, by now a small number of the police search team members had made their way down to observe the Coastguard at work, not something they saw every day, and indeed some claimed total ignorance of the skills of their local Coastguard teams.

"Shit, no way on earth would you get me to step off that edge there, even if you paid me a million pounds." Exclaimed one officer.

"I would," answered his teammate, "It's more likely to do with trust, isn't it? Trust in your team and trust in the equipment. I think they do training for this all the time as teams. One of my mates is on a cliff team down Kent way."

"Well, it is not for me." repeated the first officer, "Without being crude I would wet myself in fear or worse."

There was general silence then as Michael's blue helmet gradually disappeared from view. It was planned that he carefully lowered himself onto the next level down.

Shortly three whistle blasts were heard from down below, followed fairly quickly by four short blasts. Ropework at the top was changed, every person seemingly with their own skilled job to do. The ropes were now arranged and fed around the drum of the winch whilst they awaited more information from Michael down below.

Aled's radio gave a momentary crackle then a message from Michael stating that he was going to contact his Station Officer by landline as long as he had a signal. This in itself did not bode well for what was down below.

Aled's phone duly rang, and he looked almost furtively around as he spoke.

Huws and his DS had now arrived at the plateau, Aled waved towards them indicating that they were needed.

"What do you have for us? Has your colleague found anything?"

"Yes, indeed he has, he has found the main reason all these bloody seagulls are down there, he phoned rather than radioed as you never know who is listening, so many people have scanners these days, but there is certainly a body down there. We can send a photo with our team iPhone to our Ops room and they can forward them no doubt, to your people, or I'm perfectly happy to rig one of you up to get you down there."

Huws looked at Howard, "What do you reckon, forensic lady or you?"

"Really!" exclaimed Howard. "You want me to go down there on a rope?"

"Well, either you do or Mrs. Frosty knickers can go down if I were to tell her to."

A stern voice came from behind him.

"Ask me to, would be far more polite DI Huws if you mean me."

The subject of his name-calling was standing right behind him. Embarrassment and shame caused his face to flush red as he stuttered an apology. She chose to ignore it.

"Of course, I will go down there if my equipment can be lowered alongside me in a suitably safe bag." She said this as if it was something she may well be doing on a regular basis.

Knowing she had one up on Huws she walked towards Aled, asking to be suitably kitted out. She needed to get down there.

"What a hell of a woman," voiced Huws, more to himself than

to the open-mouthed DS standing next to him. "Well, she well and truly caught you out didn't she?" he retorted with a wink.

Aled made the decision that Michael should be winched back to the top and then if he was up to it, they would rig him up to do an accompanied descent to take the forensics lady down. She would apparently make an initial assessment and if needed would ask for her colleague to be taken down too.

The winch slowly lifted Michael back up and through the quad-pod to the top where he unclipped his gear from his harness and promptly sat down feet away from the clifftop. Both Dyfed and Aled strode across to him. He was ashen.

"Just give me a second." He demanded.

One of the police search officers offered him a bottle of water- he declined with a wave of the hand.

"I'm making a huge effort here to keep my breakfast where it is. It isn't very happy where it is at the moment and is trying to escape upwards. I will be OK in a minute." Michael, normally calm and composed was clearly shocked. He took repeated deep breaths, exhaling through pursed lips in a desperate attempt to compose himself. Whatever was down there had clearly shaken him greatly.

DI Huws and Howard had by now made their way across, Huws recognising immediately the face of a shocked man. He gave him time; he did not press him until Michael was ready to talk.

"Well, I have seen a few bodies in my service with the Coast-guard and although you never actually get used to it, this one is like nothing I've ever seen before. He is at the base of the cliff, but I'm one hundred percent certain that he has not fallen. He has been pushed over the edge after someone has-" He paused at this point, leaning back on the palms of his hands, shut his eyes, and looked to the heavens. A deep breath, and then he continued, his voice broken and unfamiliar to his colleagues.

"He has been, uhm, well, how can I describe it? He has been harvested, that's it, that is the nearest word I can think of to describe what is down there." Michael rubbed his face as if attempting to erase the picture of what he had just seen down below.

"What the hell do you mean by harvested?" demanded Huws, a little harsher than he intended. He immediately regretted his curtness and apologised.

Michael continued, disguising an annoyed glare quickly.

"He has been stripped of most of his flesh and organs, and I don't mean by carrion crows and gulls or foxes. What I have seen will haunt me. I won't forget this in a hurry. I've never witnessed anything like it!"

The Forensics officer had by now been helped into a spare cliff harness, all the metalwork ready to be attached to the various ropes.

Huws stepped across to have a word.

"He says that the body is badly mutilated." Offered Idris Huws.

"Well, I expect it will be considering it's gone forty metres or so off a cliff." She responded with impatience, keen to get on with her work.

"No, I am led to believe that the damage has been done prior to him- it is male, going over the edge. The Coastguard officer there, Michael, or Malcolm I think he is called, described him as having been harvested and that the gulls likely have created minimal damage in comparison. His eyes have gone, but that is highly likely crows and gulls."

She listened intently now with growing unease.

"Ok, let me get down there, and we will plan what we are going to do next after I've seen the body for myself. Is the same officer going to come down with me?"

"I'll ask, though I wouldn't blame the poor bugger if he refuses, he is clearly shocked." Huws set off.

"All in a day's work." She called after him, Huws thought of this as a streak of hard-faced callous indifference, but understood to a degree that it was how these people managed to do their job, day in day out.

Chapter Twenty

ALED the Coastguard station Officer for his team was chatting to his colleague when Huws got back to the little group.

Michael, by now with a tad more colour to his cheeks, insisted that he was fine to go back down, adding that he really didn't want anyone else to have to see what he had. He might take a bit of time out after today but he was adamant that he would accompany the lady down. She already seemed impatient as she looked across at them. This being said, he had no intention of looking at the body again if he could avoid it, he'd lead the way down and then look the other way whilst she did whatever needed doing.

Within minutes Michael and the forensics lady- she had not offered the courtesy of giving her name, were stood as a pair, backs to the cliff. She was assisted by Michael and his clifftop technician colleagues through the metal teepee like quadpod, and were soon balanced on their toes, on the very edge of the cliff. Michael instructed her to trust him and slowly lean backward so that they were virtually at a 75-degree angle to the cliff.

"We will just take our time and slowly walk backward. The more you lean back, the easier it is. Trust me and trust the equipment, you will be fine."

She barely nodded such was the determination and concentration on her face. She seemed not to suffer from fear, just a tough emphasis around the job at hand. Less than a minute later they were just touching the ground below. Michael whistled. The rope was slackened slightly, their feet touched the limestone slab, allowing Michael to unclip the metal descenders off the rope. They both stepped away from the cliff bottom, barely able to see the blue-helmeted heads of the men above because of the very slight overhang. Michael whistled again, to let them know that they were free of the ropes.

Michael indicated with his hand, pointing in the direction of the body, but she was already making her way towards it. He walked to the seaward side of the cliff and set his gaze on Moelfre in the distance, he could just see the promontory that was the Great Orme near LLandudno well away to the right too. Anything to take his mind off what was barely thirty feet away.

"Mm, I see exactly what you mean by 'harvested'," came her voice. Michael was not really keen to listen to a running commentary either, but unfortunately, unless he actually jumped into the water below, he had no choice but to listen to her describing her findings into her Dictaphone.

"Male, evident by the facial features and the exposed genitalia. Difficult to give an exact age, but early twenties." Her voice droned on. Michael was almost tempted to cover his ears like a child and rock himself for comfort. Although he had his back to her, every word painted the technicolour picture of what he had already seen, clear as a photograph in his mind's eye.

"Stripped naked, no footwear. Tattoo on the upper arm but not complete due to the flesh below being stripped off to the elbow.

The flesh also stripped off the other arm.

Abdominal muscle cut across in line with the ribs. A section of ribs five, six, and seven cut through, a clean-cut, so likely a hack saw or similar.

The heart was removed and missing from the chest cavity. Lungs in situ but lacerated. No doubt due to the clumsy removal of the heart.

Abdominal contents exposed; liver removed completely, spleen, pancreas, gall bladder, and intestines exposed and damaged, likely from the removal of the liver, but some indication of rough lacerations, possibly from bird or animal predation.

Upper thighs, flesh removed." She paused at this point, unbeknown to Michael, she was turning the body over sufficiently to see and confirm that his buttocks had been removed.

"Both buttocks removed. The remainder of the back is intact."

She called Michael at this point.

"I've just done a preliminary inspection here in situ. I suspect that it will be mainly his blood in the barracks building and that is likely where he was butchered, then dragged down here and dumped over the edge."

Michael, reluctant to face her. "This is beyond horrific, it's like that Anthony Hopkins film- Silence of the lambs. What animal would actually do this sort of stuff?"

She was quiet for a minute.

"Not of animal doing, this is definitely done by human hand."

"Yes, sorry, I do know that, just a figure of speech."

She nodded. "Someone totally sick in the head. We need to get this poor guy to the path lab now, though what more they will find in a post-mortem I don't know, but we can at least cross-match the blood samples and confirm the scene of the crime. I'm asking your expert opinion now, how best do we get him from here and up the cliff face?"

Michael, shook himself a little, back to a degree of professionalism.

" I think for the sake of everyone involved we should bag him down here between us, if you are happy to, and we ask the Ops room to see if the Coastguard Helicopter is available to assist us and winch him on their stretcher. We could with our gear, get him secured on a stretcher and get him up the cliff, but it's a complicated walk out, and not particularly a safe one for the team members. There is no way that we could actually get an ambulance down from the main road across two wet fields to the quarry. Well at least we might get it down here, but uphill we would need to put both our trucks in front to maybe give it a tow. There is another route out via the farm which this land is part of, but we will still not get the ambulance here. I doubt the crew would even be willing to try."

"OK, well that all makes sense." She agreed. "So can I be taken back up top now while you all get on with the next task?"

"Of course." Michael who was fairly keen to take her up, but also knowing that in all likeliness he would be coming back down to bag the corpse which she clearly intended to avoid, and then wait to assist the helicopter winchman when they came to pick it up.

The ascent was slow, the winch however making light work of pulling both up. It was just the awkwardness for Michael of having a second person virtually sitting across his knees to allow him to keep his purchase and balance on the rock face.

Aled was on the radio to the Operations room, organizing the helicopter presence, he was also quite keen to get Michael home.

Huws was in on the conversation as was Howard. Rogers and Edwards were on their way back towards their vehicles having helped the second forensics officer to pack up and take their tools of the trade back to their van. She would await the return of her senior partner.

Aled's phone rang five minutes after the helicopter request.

He chatted and nodded and chatted some more before turning to Huws.

"The helicopter is on its route back from a job in the mountains. It will refuel at Caernarfon airbase then make its way here. They've offered to drop down two of their personnel to bag and stretcher the body themselves to save Michael, from having to go down again. I know they don't know what they have let themselves in for, but they made the offer. I'm actually quite grateful for that. We'll break up our kit now and get it packed away and I'll send Michael back to the road with the flank team and Dyfed over there, and I-" he pointed towards another volunteer who was carefully removing the ropes from the winch and pulling up the blue-painted stakes that secured it to the ground.

"Dyfed and I will stay behind with our team truck until the helicopter is on its way. We've given them a grid location, but because of how the wind is affected in the proximity of the cliffs we'll put up an orange smoke canister, so the pilot can work out exactly which way to approach the job."

He added, that by all accounts of the description, he was pleased none of them had to do any more, and he was sure Michael would be just fine after a good cup of tea and perhaps something a bit stronger from behind his bar.

Aled added the last sentence without conviction, clearly concerned about Michael.

Huws at this point thanked them all and set off on his weary way back up the slope to his vehicle.

"What a day." He said to Howard, and the Forensics officer who walked along with them.

"By the way, my name is Greta Wilson." She announced. It took Huws aback; he could have sworn she had winked at him. He nodded in acknowledgment, with just the hint of a smile, then continued on his way.

The stuffing appeared to have been knocked out of everyone it seemed.

Chapter Twenty-One

MICHAEL STRODE straight to the optics behind the still closed and empty bar. A double Glenmorangie went straight into a glass. He downed it in one. Not a particular fan of a good malt, or the palate to appreciate one, he shook his head as if to cool the whisky burn hitting the back of his throat, then having barely swallowed he poured another.

He took a seat in the window alcove, knowing that the pub would normally be opening its doors in less than an hour. He made another impromptu decision; he went through to the back office and came out with a hastily written note announcing that the pub would not be opening that evening. He stuck it on the outer porch door then grabbed his phone and posted the same message on both the village community page and the pub page.

He would not make any excuses or apologies, he needed time to himself. Knowing full well some regulars may be upset, he didn't care, not tonight.

. . .

Making sure the door was firmly closed, he turned the lock and took himself upstairs to the lounge.

Chapter Twenty-Two

ALED and Dyfed both sat on a weather-worn implement of old industrial days, red with rust and flaking. If it had been another day, Aled may well have seen an artistic photo opportunity in it, particularly if Jo his wife had accompanied him for a walk. However, this small bay and quarry did not particularly entice him to visit, having already retrieved what was left of a body from here the previous year.

Dyfed was deep in his own thoughts, both men awaiting the distant thrumming of the rotors of the Coastguard Sikorsky S-92 helicopter. Likely it would appear overhead from behind them, coming as it was from Caernarfon on the mainland, South West of them.

Neither Dyfed nor Aled had seen the horror below them and considering they were fairly hardened to multiple sad sights, neither of them wanted to etch the apparent appalling image onto the inside of their eyeballs, never to be removed. It had been enough to listen to Michael's report on the phone. Aled had not even fully described the scene to Dyfed. The less that knew the better.

Aled's phone pinged. Their group WhatsApp messenger. He glanced. Ceri had heard that she had missed a call, wanting to know what was 'Kicking off' and was it worth her coming over. Was she needed?

Aled almost chose to ignore the request, knowing it was also a bit of a dig for details. He thanked her for the offer but replied that they were fine and that the job was coming to its conclusion.

They were roused from their contemplations by the distant sound of the rescue helicopter. Dyfed jumped up grabbing the small pull-top can that was next to him. He looked back at the cliff face and seeing the red and white helicopter appearing, he moved towards the edge of the cliff in front of them and pulled the ring on the can. This gave him a few seconds of leeway to place it on the ground. Vast clouds of bright orange smoke appeared, rising on the wind.

A cliff approach was always difficult, whether they were mountains or high sea stacks. The wind would waft in from the sea and race around the cliff to be spat out somewhere else causing confusing turbulence. The helicopter flew over out to sea, then turned and carefully manouvered itself nose to wind. The two men could feel the downdraught and pulled down their goggles and covered their noses and mouths with their Coastguard issue fluorescent buffs. Gravel and general small debris flew all around them.

Due to the fact that the ledge where the body was jutted out below them, the helicopter was barely above their heads as they stood on the ledge above.

The pilot gave them a thumbs up whilst the winchman was helped out of the side by another crewman. He was coming down with a stretcher. A black bag strapped onto it in preparation for the task.

Dyfed watched the winchman dropping down out of sight and then hear over the comms that he was on the ground and releasing himself from his harness. He added that it was quite likely that he would be able to place the deceased into the stretcher himself after placing him in a body bag, negating the need for a second crewman to descend.

The helicopter moved away, hovering a good half-mile away out at sea, reducing the force of the downdraught whilst the unpleasant task was being carried out below.

The radio broke into voice, the job was done, bagged, and secured in the stretcher, the winchman requested the return of the helicopter to lift.

The huge machine came back into position. The crewmember releasing the winch cable and attempting to guide its descent towards his colleague.

Neither Aled nor Dyfed had a visual of the goings-on below, but within seconds the Winchman and the laden stretcher was lifting in front of them, twisting slightly in the wind and downdraught as it got nearer the side door. Had it been a normal job they may both have held a highline attached to the helicopter to prevent any over spin of the stretcher as it was lifted up. Today the crew had to just take their chance.

The stretcher was pulled in, another thumbs up from the pilot and a steep swoop to the left took them circling over the bay and back in the direction of Bangor hospital.

"Shit, that was not the most pleasant of jobs." Declared Dyfed.

"No, and we didn't even have to look at the poor bugger, but Michael won't sleep for a fucking month now after what he saw."

Dyfed looked towards his colleague in agreement but also taken aback, having never heard his well-mannered Accountant colleague utter an expletive in all the time he had volunteered alongside him. He stepped forward to carefully touch the smoke canister lest it still be hot. He picked it up still warm and followed Aled back across the plateau towards the truck. Aled followed the by now muddy furrows with difficulty, but not wanting to create more tracks than there already were for the poor landowner. He had appeared earlier to watch his field cut up.

Not a word was spoken until they pulled up in the small car park behind the village pub. Michael had already sent a text inviting them for a coffee before returning to the station.

Chapter Twenty-Three

EMYR ROWLANDS HAD BEEN NOTIFIED by his friend Idris that a helicopter would be incoming shortly, bringing a second body in for him to have a look at. An ambulance had already been sent to the helipad for the transfer. The description was gruesome. 'Cannibalistic' was the word that Idris had chosen to use. Idris was on his way across, adding that he would be alone in the observation room as he was not very keen to share the stomach-churning images he was soon to see with his younger team cohorts.

Greta Wilson described to him what she said was an unforgettable shocking image. She added that in her career she had seen many a ghastly death, but nothing like this. He was not looking forwards to this autopsy at all.

Huws arrived at the suite at the same time as a porter was wheeling in a trolley on which lay the stretcher with the bagged corpse atop. He was whistling away cheerfully; little did he know what he was pushing, barely slowing to knock open the swinging double doors, stating to Jane and Emyr that the Helicopter crew wanted the stretcher back so, "Can you take the body off please? They're in a hurry to get off again."

With practiced ease they slid a hard plastic board under one side of the body bag on the stretcher and in one move pulled it across the shiny board until it was on the stainless steel autopsy table. These tables with their slopes and drains and headrests were a far cry from the old slate slabs that Idris had been familiar with in the early days of his service.

DI Huws took himself off to the short flight of stairs that led to the observation room. He was quite taken aback to find that it was already occupied by a small group of student doctors. He could virtually smell the nervousness in the room.

"Good evening," said Huws, introducing himself. "I presume you have attended a few of these by now? Are you aware of the nature of this autopsy?" he added.

As nervous nods and a few stuttered explanations that this was to be their first, Huws felt sorry for the lot of them. Experience told him that of the six in the room, likely three at least would not see this particular autopsy to its end. Huws settled himself down, sliding his hand up after groveling in his pocket and put a mint imperial in his mouth, he offered the bag around. There were no takers. "You should take one, they will distract you." Though as soon as he said those words, he knew that only a blindfold would distract them in this instance.

Huws suddenly got up and pushed the communication button, "By the way we believe that the young man is called Simon Chatterris." Rowlands nodded. "The first one was called Christopher Tennant. He was obviously trying to indicate that his friend Simon here was in trouble. We know where the crime scene was, regarding this young guy, but we believe it possible that the first victim was maybe chased towards, and fatally injured nearer to the village. Very likely going for help. The location is barely a mile away but would you agree that those injuries may have caused him to bleed out way before he reached the village?"

Emyr Rowlands paused in his work electric saw in hand.

"Yes, I have to agree, I doubt anyone could have walked or run that far with those injuries. I predict that he would have bled out internally within around eight minute. I would suggest that you get some search personnel to walk, run, for a maximum of eight minutes from where he was found and search a radius of around two hundred metres or so from there to see if you find anything. Anyway, I digress, that's your job."

He placed the saw against the skull and removed a cap-like section of the skull.

Huws knew that in this case, although the injuries were obvious, Rowlands would be meticulous in his method. Despite the injuries, they still theoretically needed a cause of death.

Step by careful step he worked down the body, a running commentary as he went. Jane recorded and weighed the remaining removed organs, and step by brisk step the young student medics looked increasingly peaky, vacated their seats, and exited the room. Huws had been wrong, only two stuck it out to the bitter end, all credit to them he thought.

Rowlands after a laborious almost two hours looked towards Huws in the gallery and nodded a request for him to come down. Huws nodded and smiled at the two remaining medical students who were the same pallor as the lab coats. "Well done for sticking it out."

Rowlands was already pulling off his gloves. He met him in the corridor and Huws followed him into his office.

"A tot?" he asked.

"Go on then, I shouldn't but I'm going to go home from here. There is nothing really I want to set the teams doing until they've had a nights rest, and we can reconvene with a new plan in the morning."

He took the cut glass whisky tumbler from Rowlands hand who clearly hadn't considered the answer would be anything other than a yes.

"Cause of death?" questioned Idris.

"To be honest, it is difficult to decide. There is no apparent head injury, so I've eliminated the possibility of blunt head trauma. The removal of flesh and the organs would obviously have led to his death but what the initial injury was, to be totally honest, I can't tell you. I'm hoping to God he was dead before he was stripped inside and out, you said that there was a huge amount of blood inside the old building?"

Huws nodded.

"Well, I would suggest that it's likely he suffered a possible fatal stab wound dealt by the same pitchfork as our first victim. Maybe this lad was fatally injured rendering him immobile whilst the second lad was, despite the injuries inflicted on him, able to run and get away." Rowlands looked at his old friend. Just total speculation though at this stage."

"That is perfectly plausible I suppose. Whoever has carried out this atrocity must be a fairly big person to be able to overpower two young lads," added Huws into the mix.

"Not if they had both been asleep at the time. Maybe they dossed down in the shed for shelter for the night, which means that it is likely that they were actually seen making their way down there."

Rowlands assumptions made sense but as Idris Huws under-stood, speculation got you nowhere, they needed facts that could be made into proof.

Idris paused, and looked at his old friend. Hardly daring to voice the question that was on the tip of his tongue.

"Silly question, I know, but here goes, there is no way that this could have been done by that bloody big cat that was around a couple of years ago could it?"

Rowlands gave the smallest hint of a smile.

"Well, when we find a cat who understands anatomy and is able to systematically strip a human body of organs and flesh with what is obvious to anyone, a very sharp knife, then, no Idris, I don't believe this has been done by a pitchfork-wielding panther or any other cat for that matter."

"Hmm, I know, I know, I just wanted to be happy in myself, but there is one thing at the back of my mind that bothers me. There were three victims during the cat incidents. One of them a reported missing from home person, was found down in the very same bay, skeletal remains, but could this be down to the same killer as opposed to an overdose death and natural decomposition." Huws was awaiting his friend's response.

"Quite a possibility, I can dig out the file pertaining to that incident and have a look at the findings again. I suggest you go home and get yourself something to eat. I think you have a busy time ahead of you." Rowlands turned towards the door as his assistant Jane entered the room. Jane spoke directly to Huws. A distinct familiarity in her words and tone.

"Get yourself home Idris, and make sure you eat something sensible, don't just fill up on crap and keep in touch over the next few days, you know, it's good to talk. Pop over when you are able."

She strode across to the sideboard and took the kettle off its stand and left to fill it for a much-needed cup of tea. She had not yet fallen into the habit of a whisky after every autopsy.

Chapter Twenty-Four

DI IDRIS HUWS did not get much sleep that night, he was rarely one for dreams and nightmares, it was more that he couldn't actually get off to sleep. He saw his ancient bedside digital clock display each and every hour until four am. He tossed and turned, made plans for the morning, changed his mind, made a few more until he believed he had something workable to put in front of his young detectives in the morning.

He had a phone call to attend to as soon as he set foot in his office. His DCI wanted a word. No doubt, complaining about the cost of resourcing the investigation as was his tendency. Huws despaired sometimes that he behaved as if the money was actually being taken out of the Chief's own bank account. He was grateful though that his superior was pretty much desk-bound out of choice, whiling away his last year before retirement. He did give Huws a relative amount of freedom to drive his own bus and take charge, that at least was something to be thankful for.

On the dot of four am he reached for his phone which was charging on the bedside cabinet and scrolled along to find the BBC Radio app that Jane had introduced him to. He had only used it a couple of times to listen to a podcast. He couldn't listen to music or any drama with raucous fake laughter, so he chose a Radio Four current affairs programme. Inevitably and as guaranteed by Jane, he never heard the end of any programme as his mind drifted into sleep. He had an early start the next morning. Lots to organize, happy that his plan was set, he set his phone alarm and drifted off to an episode of You and Yours.

Arriving in the incident room later that morning, he was pleased to see that his team were already there.

Justin Howard was in fact in the act of pinning a whole set of photographs onto the Perspex wall. Jane, fair play, must have worked into the night to write up the autopsy report and send the photos through.

A small crowd of officers were standing behind Justin, each new photograph bought exclamations of shock, and disbelief, particularly from the youngest ones. They had wanted to see them and not, in equal measure.

"Christ Almighty, no wonder that poor Coastguard officer who went down the cliff looked ashen and virtually collapsed when he came back up the cliff. The poor bloke went back down too with the forensics bod."

Edwards had witnessed the blood in the barracks but not in his wildest imaginings had he realised that this sort of shocking damage had been bestowed on the victim. He immediately regretted looking.

Huws allowed Justin to pin up all the photos, and when the team appeared to have their fill of the horror and started returning to their desks, he explained.

"At this moment in time, we have no real evidence of the exact cause of death, we know the young man likely bled out and died in the barracks building.

I think, and this is merely speculation, that he was then butchered right where he had fallen and then dragged to the clifftop inside the remnants of their green tent and his remains pushed over the cliff. Maybe the killer was not fully aware of the depth front to back of the ledge below, and just assumed he would land in the sea.

Seems he then made an attempt to burn the tent on the clifftop.

Our first Victim Christopher may well have been attacked whilst trying to fight off the killer, either off himself or when attempting to help his friend Simon.

Anyway, he got away, his injuries were fatal according to the pathologist, but evidently he must have been supremely strong and determined. The killer may have been confident that he would not get far, not far enough to be found and blow his cover, and got back to the job of butchering Simon, probably with the intention of dealing with him later.

To add to this now, I am suspecting that the skeletal remains that were discovered high on the pebble beach down there, is it three, nearly four years ago now, may well have met the same demise. So, whether this killer is local, or an opportunist which I find very difficult to believe, I now firmly believe they are linked. Mr. Emyr Rowlands will find the autopsy file relating to the death of our skeleton, so see if our initial findings could actually be attributed to a similar modus operandi." Huws looked at his team, from one to another- murmurs of agreement passed between them. This path however may well be a dead end.

"Meanwhile." He continued knowing that he again had their full attention.

"Meanwhile, Rowlands has deducted that if the young man Christopher had been attacked on route to where he finally fell then he would no doubt have succumbed to his loss of blood in no longer than around eight minutes, which also could indicate that he got away, maybe only slightly injured but was then followed by the killer and attacked further. What this means is that I want someone who can walk from the spot where Christopher was found, back in the direction of the quarry, for a maximum of ten minutes to see where that gets us too. It's not rocket science but it is all we have got.

It may actually lead us to another spot where we may find more evidence of an attack." Huws didn't add that with the amount of holes in the poor lad, he likely bled like a sieve and must therefore have left further evidence behind somewhere.

"He punctured some internal organs which would have caused

major bleeds, the damage to his lungs would also have seriously debilitated him very quickly too.

"So, the plan today is to do this timed walk, followed by the search teams moving out from the supposed spot, either side of the road to see if anything is found. We are assuming that he took the most direct route from the quarry, but they no doubt arrived from the East and may have been unfamiliar with the pathway continuing to the west and towards the village."

The team babbled amongst themselves, deciding who was going to take on the walk.

DS Howard, although fully understanding all the implications, pointed out that he and Edwards would like to pop out and just visit the last two properties that they had not been to regarding the pitchforks.

"I know that after yesterday and being called out to the second body, the forensics will be behind in their testing of the pitchfork handles already in their possession, but if there was a chance there are a couple more, then my database would be complete. I'd also like to request a warrant to be issued as I envisage maybe that Mr. William Evans- do you remember him? Grumpy old bissum? He was the father of Ashley Evans the drug runner who was shot last year, in the incident involving Littleton? I suspect he'll make it difficult for us to look around," he paused for his DI's response.

"Of course, I remember him, just go carefully there. He was a right cantankerous fellow, but then again, we did go there to tell him his estranged son was a big-time drug dealer and was dead. More than likely just full of bluster and hot air."

"Yes we will take care, but I'm just pre-empting his refusal to give us access, so it will save wasting time if we are prepared."

Plans made, everyone got on with the tasks for the day. Edwards would once again accompany DS Howard to the farm searches. They were going to leave Evans's property till after they had cleared the first, in anticipation of things not running as smoothly as hoped with Evans.

Rogers was taking a team member with her, she had chosen him specifically due to him being of similar build and height to Christopher Tennant, she and Huws who had chosen to accompany her would see where the walk ended in order to coordinate the Police Search and Rescue teams again, through their head of operations.

Firstly, he would pop into the pub in Allt Goch on his way through, just to have a chat with Michael the landlord and out of decency check up on his wellbeing.

Chapter Twenty-Five

JUSTIN HOWARD and Griff Edwards had finished in their first property and despite a good look around the outbuildings with the owner, no pitchforks or anything similar had been found. The owner's workshop was immaculate, everything in its designated place, a name sticker for every single tool and implement and apart from that, cleaned as if new. Justin had actually asked Griff three times if he was ready to leave. Who would have known that Griff in his spare time was a woodworking buff as well as a vintage vehicle enthusiast?

They laughed at his obsession as they made their way to the next farm belonging to Mr. William Evans. Neither anticipating an easy job but Griff excited by opportunity of having a look around the old barns and sheds.

"Can't wait to have a nosey around the old boy's sheds, you never know what gems you might find."

"Yes, you have mentioned this a few times before." Laughed Justin. "Just you make sure you concentrate on the job in hand and don't be trying to haggle with him and buying loads of crap, you can do that in your free time."

"Ha, don't worry, I won't. I will have my concentration fully on pitchforks only." Griff was pleased to have a bit of banter with Justin, good to hear him laugh, and that smile returning to his face. He and the team had been saddened to see his decline over the last months and were at a loss as to how to help him. Justin however had chosen slowly and surely to shut them all out. Griff felt sorry for him.

Griff Edwards took a chance. "Do you fancy coming for a pint this evening if we finish at a reasonable time, and nothing pressing appears?"

Justin barely glancing across, muttered "Uhm, no thanks, I have a lot of work to be going on with, but thanks for the offer."

Griff knew better than to pursue the conversation.

"How long were you and Steff together for?" A change of subject.

"Not long enough." Another door closed firmly in Griff's face.

They continued the short journey to the next property in silence.

The drive had not improved since their last visit, slowly advancing towards the farm buildings with the sole aim of not catching the sump or the exhaust on the rims of crater-like holes. Some filled with alloy scratching stones and general pieces of old long worn cement.

"We'll give the door a knock together and see how he welcomes us, or not as might be the case. We have a warrant, but let's just see if we can persuade him to let us do this the easy way with no fuss." Justin was already stepping out of the car as he continued- "If he is happy to let us have a look around the buildings, best stick together, so keep your wits about you, don't go drifting off on your own vintage tractor search."

"Right boss." Griff was a tad miffed that he was considered not professional enough to give his task his full attention, but he let it go, a step behind Justin, they approached the back door and knocked.

No response was heard, Justin knocked again, harder, Edwards, by now stepping away from the door heard a creak from within the house and a dull thud.

"Is there another door on the other side? I have a feeling that

Mr. Evans is avoiding us and leaving by the front, or back door, whichever it may be."

Before Howard could respond Edwards had turned tail and made his way around the corner of the house.

"Hey, hang on there, I said to stay together."

Edwards barely paused in acknowledgment of his senior officer's orders, he had by now glimpsed Evans making his way across the unkempt orchard that was at the front of the property and making his way to a small gate to the field beyond.

"Sir, hang on there, we only want a word with you, I appreciate you farmers are busy, but can we have a few minutes of your time?"

The dishevelled figure turned to face Edwards, Howard now hot on his heels and pushing himself ahead of his colleague. "Might we have a quick word? We'll try to be as quick as we can?"

The man muttered a reluctant yes.

Edwards turned to Howard, "Uhm Sir," Howard cut him short and ignored him.

"We would like to have a look through your sheds if we may."

"Sir?" Edwards again. Once again Howard continued, clearly annoyed at the butting in.

"You may have heard on the local grapevine or radio that we were holding an amnesty in the local area?"

"I don't see anyone and have no wireless or television." Responded Evans brusquely.

"We're checking farms for any implements and tools that may have been used and possibly dumped in the local area. Would you give permission for us to do a search? I have to say at this point that we have got a warrant for this purpose, but it is always more pleasant for all concerned if we can do this amicably."

The old man still glowered, muttering under his breath.

"I suppose I have no choice do I? I expect you to have put everything back exactly as you found it. I'm off for a walk."

At this juncture, Howard was bemused to notice that his walk was to be accompanied by a handful of sheets of newspaper. He did not want to imagine the purpose of the walk. At least you would be out of the way for the purpose of their visit, or at least for most of it.

Edwards was keen to get his penn'orth in.

"Did you see what he had on his feet?"

"Well, no, I didn't in that undergrowth, why?" Howard asked.

"Black Salomon walking trainers. Strange purchase for a guy like that, but more notably, the same make and colour of the missing shoes of our quarry victim."

"Shit, really? Are you sure?"

"Bit of a coincidence don't you think?"

Howard paused to think, "Right, come on, we know he is otherwise occupied for a little while, let's just start at that smaller shed over there, it could well be a workshop but let's just call this in. I'll let the DI know. In fact, he is not that far up the road somewhere walking a timed route for our first victim. He can get a team together and send over here as a backup. As long as we just behave normally it won't arouse any suspicion on his part that we have concerns about him."

Edwards nodded his agreement and attempted to loosen the rusted bolt shutting the warped wooden door of the chosen shed, the wood twisted enough to cause the bolt to be stiff and tight. Howard was already on his radio, Edwards able to hear the other side of the conversation in his earpiece. Orders to stay where they were and not antagonize Evans in any way, should he show his face before more personnel arrived, Huws was also preparing to organize the firearms team to respond who would make way when they could.

Howard shone his torch towards both walls each side of the door looking for a light switch, Edwards pointing out to him its pointlessness as he shone his own torch towards smashed fragments of glass in the bulb holder above, his attention having been drawn by the crush of glass fragments under his boot.

This workshop was poles apart from the farm they had visited this morning. Tools, piled up against the wall in a drunken higgledy-piggledy fashion, wood and iron, no organization, no care. A solid wooden workbench had a collection of hand tools which certainly by the evidence seen around them of abandonment and general dereliction, had not been used for a number of years, a lathe and a band saw dressed in a veil of cobwebs stood sadly in a corner, possibly a sign of a previous life of busyness and pride in workmanship. Maybe even a previous generation. There was no pride in this place now for sure. Justin noted that Griff was thoroughly inspecting things, clearly as much from personal interest as from a police perspective. Hebshook his head and grinned to himself just as his head whipped around at the sound of the bolt being closed on the door.

"Hey, Mr. Evans, we're still in here, can you open the door again, we will be as quick as we can. Mr. Evans?"

Howard looked towards Griff Edwards, barely able to make out a shape in the dark. Edwards torch burst into light, dazzling Howard.

There was no answer from outside and no opening of the door. Howard rubbed his hand over his chin, anxiety clear to see on his face.

"What now?" Edwards asked. Howard was already at the door giving it his best shoulder push.

He repeated his request for Evans to open it, convinced already that it had not been shut in error.

"Mr. Evans, this will do no good locking us in here, the sooner we can eliminate you from our inquiries, as we have done everyone else this last few days, the sooner we can leave you in peace."

Edwards was now shining his light furiously at the workbench beside him.

"Help me look for anything useful we could use to take these doors off the hinges, there must be something here.

Howard had broken out into a cold sweat, until that precise moment in time he had not realised that he suffered from claustrophobia, it wasn't every day that he was locked in a dark shed by someone who increasingly looked like a madman. He heard rustling by the door.

"Evans, open the door." Demanding now, the pleasantries of a Mr. discarded.

"Come on man, just be sensible and open the door, let's not let things get unpleasant."

"Shit." Edwards was drawing his attention to the disappearing light under the door. The rustling had been Evans stuffing newspaper into the gaps. Liquid followed. A strong smell now of fuel.

"Diesel," said Edwards. "Still flammable, but let's hope the wood of the door is damp enough that he can't ignite it like petrol would. There was a whoosh, the gap reopened and allowed light in, clearly and thankfully the paper had burnt, but he had failed to light the old door. They could hear more liquid being sloshed, a click of a lighter, some smoke now making its way under the door.

Edwards appeared behind Howard and threw a bucket of water at the base of the door.

"Where the hell did that come from?" demanded Howard.

"In the corner, sat catching drips from that hole in the roof."

Howard nodded, sweat beading on his brow.

Edwards sensed his senior partner's fear.

"We'll be fine boss, don't worry, even if he manages to light it, I'm sure the team will be here in no time at all."

No more smoke appeared. No sounds at all came from outside, the door remained firmly closed.

They stood behind the door, Howard in silence listening out for any sounds of approaching vehicles, his throat was in his mouth, his breath ragged and fast, hurting his chest. His heart was trying to escape his chest such was its pounding. He knew he was building up to one of his panic attacks. This was the last thing he wanted to happen at work. He had suffered plenty of them since losing Steff, but only ever in the privacy of his own home. His fingers were starting to tingle, he knew he needed to control his breathing. He was becoming desperate, he felt faint.

Edwards stood in front of him. "Justin mate, Justin, look at me."

He took hold of Justin's hands in his own.

"Listen, make a fist of your hand, take as big a breath as you can, and blow against your forefinger and thumb while you make that fist. Blow for five seconds, come on, do it."

"What the hell?" demanded Howard but did as he was told.

"Now count to five and do it again." Howard obeyed.

Edwards insisted this continued until Howards' breathing became nearer normal, and he started to calm down.

"Well done mate, my sister used to have panic attacks and a paramedic that turned out to her once got her to do this. It does help."

Howard nodded his appreciation and simultaneously they both turned their heads in response to the sound of vehicles entering the farmyard. Doors slamming closed. Huws calling.

"Howard, Edwards, where are you?"

"Not a word to the others please." Pleaded Howard as he touched Edwards arm. "I'll get this under control, I promise. Our secret?"

Edwards felt akin to a primary school child sharing a secret with his best friend which had been passed under a desk on a notebook page corner. But for the time being he agreed it would stay between them.

"DI Huws, Sir, we are here," shouted Edwards. Turning to face the doors as feet approached from outside. Someone clearly struggling as they had to slide open the rusty seized bolt.

Chapter Twenty-Six

LIGHT FLOODED the building as the wooden door was swung open. Justin Howard almost fell out, feeling the need to gasp at the air as if hungry. DI Idris Huws stood directly in front of him and instinct drew in to place both hands on a shoulder, virtually holding Justin up.

"I'm fine Sir, honestly, just the smoke."

Huws glanced over Howard's shoulders noticing the fragment of now wet newspapers under the door, barely enough to have created a single wisp. However, he knew this was far more than that.

"You're fine now in the fresh air, just slow down your breathing, it will help clear the smoke," he nodded vigorously as he spoke, Howard looking him in the eye for the first time and mimicking his nodding, understanding full well that his boss recognized the panic that had clearly overtaken him but at the same time protecting him from actually pointing it out. Edwards had similarly fallen into an unspoken plan and had a hand against the wall pretending to struggle to breathe in support of his colleague.

"Good thing we found the bucketful of stinky stagnant water to throw at the door- it put the fire out very quickly, so lucky."

Howard responded with a nod and appeared to compose himself.

"Did anyone see Evans as you drove in?"

"Don't worry lad, we have a few men on foot already doing a quick search for him across his farmland, I've sent one officer to the top of Bwrdd Arthur over there which may give us a vantage point if he is making his way towards the quarry. We we'll find him and bring him in for questioning. Did you say he was wearing our victims walking boots?"

Edwards responded.

"Yes I believe so Sir, a pair of black Salomons, decent shoes, probably purchased online, so unless he has a computer or laptop to use, then I would put my next salary cheque on them belonging to Simon Chatterris."

Huws nodded thoughtfully "Did you pay attention to any of his other clothing?"

"Well actually not really Sir, but I do believe that he was wearing black trousers. He appeared to be walking somewhere to perform his ablutions, newspaper in hand."

"Mm, well, we know now what he did with the newspaper don't we."

Huws turned to the officers that had driven in and gathered behind him. A van had appeared out of which a large long-haired German Shepherd dog was bouncing out, full of enthusiasm for its next task, its handler holding the loops of the longest black web lead that Edwards had seen.

"Is this man likely to be armed?" called the handler.

"No idea, but assume that he may well be." Responded Huws.

The handler made towards the house door, the one that he was informed that Evans had left the property by, he would start his search from there.

Huws turned to the other officers; they were awaiting his instructions.

"You lot get the rest of these sheds checked over, continue what DS Howard and Edwards were doing. Any implements or hand tools that could match up with the instrument used as a weapon for both our victims. We'll have a look in the house."

Howard nodded, having composed himself but still appearing pale. He nodded towards the house whilst indicating with his hand that Edwards should follow himself and Huws indoors.

"You OK now mate?" asked Edwards.

"Not your mate." Was the curt reply that came his way. At least he understood where he stood.

"No sir, sorry Sir." He followed his superiors towards the back door.

"We better glove up I suppose." Huws already pulling a pair of gloves out of his jacket pocket, Howard did the same. Edwards patted his pockets and declared he had arrived unprepared.

"Don't worry, have these." Huws pulled a second pair out of his pocket.

The door opened creakily, straight into a long low roofed room, that could only be described as an outhouse. A slate slab suspended on red brick pillars barely visible such was the collection of household and farm detritus covering its surface. No doubt in the early years of this home's life, the slate slab would have been immaculately polished and used as a cold store for meats and dairy products from the animals that would have enjoyed the pastures outside.

The door at the side led into the main house, Edwards held his nose, an unpleasant odour of stale urine and indescribable stench assaulted their senses.

"Jeez, this place is making my eyes water, God help my allergies, must be all sorts in here." Edwards cautiously moved into what appeared to be the only used room so far in the house, an old threadbare spring erupting armchair, the horsehair stuffing escaping the well-worn arms. Hessian sacking draped over the back imitating a sad stained antimacassar. The thin carpet was indistinguishable from the floor, so covered was it in papers and general household waste. The source of the eye-watering stench was discovered around the walls in the presence of cat faeces in various stages of dryness. The odd, skeletal carcass a rat lay sadly under a three-legged table which was balanced upon three colourful milk crates- the only brightness in the room. Another skeleton, this one more recent as its dried mummified sightless head was still attached, this time a rabbit. DS Howard put his head around the door of the downstairs toilet and rapidly retreated, the pan was full to the brim of crusted over faeces, no doubt the result of blockages and collapsed drains in years gone by.

Edwards then piped up. "Look at this, it's no wonder the poor bugger was going out into the fields to relieve himself, he's filled all the containers that he seems to have owned with what I suspect from their colour is poo." He chose the childish word poo over anything else he may have used in deference to his senior officers.

"He has stored it all on every step of his stairs, all down one side."

"Christ, why would you keep your own shit?" asked Howard, not in the least concerned regarding his choice of word.

"I've seen this before in my time, one old lady had asked a local shopkeeper to keep all the empty ice cream cartons for her after he had dished out his thousands of summer 99's. When she died, she had filled every single one to within an inch from the top and stored them all in her dining room. She had even dated them." Huws imparted this information to an open-mouthed Edwards.

"You would do well to lift your jaw off the floor young man," looking at Edwards, "They say that smells have airborne particulates that you can absorb."

At this juncture Edwards pulled a hanky out of his trouser pocket, vigorously blew his nose and simultaneously retched.

"Hey steady on, no puking on my watch." Huws understood the likelihood that neither DS Howard or DC Edwards would have yet to witness such a property. It was certainly not his first.

"Seems he may have cooked here in his sitting room, if you can call it that. This old oven in the fireplace is likely original. I reckon he must be immune from any sort of food poisoning though by the look of this old iron pan." Huws continued to scan his surroundings before declaring there was not much to help them indoors and that they should see how the lads were getting on outside.

As they stepped outside into the welcome light and fresh air, an officer stepped into view from the corner of the house and asked Huws to follow him. Something of interest may have been found, but they did not want to move it.

Edwards was glad to get out of the house, a distinct feeling of crawling insects up his trouser legs and nape of his neck made him desperate to undress there and then and find a hosepipe to wash himself down. So convinced he was covered in cat fleas or even human lice or whatever they were, he had decided he would undress in his garage at the end of the shift and maybe even bin his clothes. He wafted his hand for the hundredth time through his hair in a desperate bid to dislodge any creatures that may be planning to feast on his blood.

DI Huws and Howard had already disappeared out of sight by the time he had finished flapping.

He joined them near the remains of a small bonfire, a few branches partly burnt down to ash, but amongst the rotting burnt branches was visible a cleaner length of wood, just around eight inches but obvious by its smoothness that it was a handle of some sort.

Huws produced an evidence bag from a pocket.

Edwards chanced a smile as he realised why his boss had a coat with so many pockets.

Huws carefully pulled the likely remains of a wooden handle out of the cold damp ash and placed it just as it was in the bag.

"I think our new friend Greta Wilson may find something of interest on this," referring to the recent softening of the local forensic pathologists' attitude towards him.

"Could this be a pitchfork -" Howard did not complete the sentence due to another officer who had been busy around them poking around with his staff looking for anything else of interest in the ground around them.

"Sir, over here, there is some metal sticking out of the ground and I would say definite footprints around it, it looks to be the part of a tool like a spade or something that fits onto the shaft of a wooden handle, could well be our pitchfork."

"Good spot officer," said Huws striding across, wishing he had put on a pair of wellies as the bottom of his trousers got increasingly wet in the long damp grass.

"Wow, that was a good spot, you can barely see it," said a by now calmer and more composed Howard. "Looks like it has been pushed right down into the earth."

The officer responded, "Well, I can't take credit for brilliant eyesight, in fact, I caught my toe in it and tripped."

"OK, how do we best get this out?" asked Huws.

"Well, I reckon, I might just be able to get the tip of my staff just under the arch of the pitchfork, someone has clearly tried to push it right down with his heel, but not quite managed to push it in completely, they probably thought it highly unlikely that anyone would find it."

The officer got down on one knee and worked at the soft soil until he was able to force the end of his pole underneath the now clear arch. He asked his colleague to grasp one end of the pole and slowly but surely the iron fork exposed itself out of the clinging ground bit by bit.

Another evidence bag was produced by Huws. Edwards laughing to himself expected him at the next plunge into the depths of his pockets to bring out a white rabbit.

The fork was placed directly into the bag, rusted red with age and now coated in a cloying covering of wet soil.

"Will there be anything to find on this after it's been in the ground?" asked Edwards.

"If this is our weapon then I'm confident that there will still be traces to be found. If we can then link it with our victims I think we may have our man; if we can find him."

Chapter Twenty-Seven

BARELY THE DISTANCE of two fields away William Evans was skulking around the back of a pretty, nineteen-thirties style bungalow. The house appeared empty. It had decking and a hot tub, not that he had ever seen one up close before. Could have been to dip sheep in as far as he was concerned. The garden was full to the brim of baskets and tubs filled with seasonal plants. No doubt the work of a keen or professional gardener. His ex-wife had been green-fingered, but he imagined as he looked around, that his lack of interest in such things had no doubt soured her enthusiasm. Over time that sourness had extended to him, bickering, belittling, griping at every little thing. Their short marriage had run its course very quickly but not before he had got her pregnant.

He thought back to that day, where he had taken her totally against her will as he still believed was his right as a husband, when constant refusal and rejection had finally pushed him as far as a man could go. He had much, much later seen the error of his ways and begged forgiveness. But she had claimed his apologies were empty of sincerity and honesty. In reflection, she was probably right. He hardly ever got to see his son apart from the year before he died, he wanted to store his ill-gotten gains in his shed. That had only led to his untimely death, but he supposed that was the risk you took if your life moved over into the criminal world.

A sound bought him out of his daydream, just a horse neighing in a nearby field. He continued his way around the cottage, all the blinds open, allowing him to recognize that the house was empty. Likely a holiday home and maybe not yet in the full swing of bookings due to the aftermath and disruption of that virus that people in town were going on about though it hadn't bothered him in the least.

Despite his wrongdoings of the last few years, he had not been raised to be a burglar. As ludicrous as that thought was he chose not to break in. He saw a blue painted summer house at the end of the garden, maybe it would be unlocked.

William Evans wondered to himself how different his life would have been if he had trodden a different path after his schooldays, and not just stuck to the shackles of the family farm. The untimely death of his parents followed by the ugly divorce changed not just the course of his life but his attitudes towards it.

The shed was open, a shed in reality that had raised itself into the realms of a summer house simply by the addition of double glass doors and a veranda. There were pretty blinds on the window. The smell of the pinewood barely disguised by containers of pot-pour-ri and the, to him, slightly sickening smell of partly burnt scented candles. The two armchairs were bedecked by a quality old Welsh tapestry blanket. Blankets favoured by his mother and her mother before her. The family would have all benefited from their warmth on their beds, but as a child, he hated the scratchiness of the wool.

. . .

He took a seat having carefully shut the door behind him. There was no key, so he knew he was unlikely to be able to stay there undiscovered for long.

He regretted his stupidity now. He ought to have just let the police have their search for the bloody pitchforks in the sheds and be done with it. They would not likely find the one he had hidden, but he knew his actions now would cause the whole thing to spiral out of his control. He had a very close shave when they found the drugs his son had hidden in his chest freezer of all places, he was unsure now how things would pan out. He sat and tried to formulate a plan in his head of how he was going to get out of this corner that he had put himself in. A short rest and a nap may well refresh him a little, though he was hungry, the pangs, creating pains across his abdomen. He couldn't remember when he had last eaten a decent meal like his mother would have fed him. A meat-only diet obviously could not be totally healthy, his guts told him that often enough.

Chapter Twenty-Eight

ROGERS HAD BEEN CALLED AWAY from the common by Huws, he wanted to meet her at the farm in order to plan their next move. The search priority now having changed from finding the location of Christopher Tennant's attack to actually planning a search for a possible perpetrator.

Rogers couldn't believe her ears when she arrived at the farm and heard of the developments.

"Are you OK Justin?" were the first words out of her mouth, seemingly unconcerned whether Griff Edwards was also unharmed.

"I'm fine thank you," he uttered, brushing aside the comment, though Edwards standing directly behind him indicated with a shake of the head that a different answer may have been more truthful. The team were still very much aware that their DS was still fragile even many months on. She would try to have a chat with him later on in the office if she got chance.

Huws turned to Howard and Edwards, "Can you take the evidence bags straight to Bangor for me? Ask them to rush them through. If they find remnants of prints or blood on either the wood or the ironwork I think we may well have a match with one or both of our victims. I want the rest of the team to have a damn good look around for any other tools that he may have used to cut Simon Chatterris up, as that certainly wasn't done with the fork, we need to maybe find a knife, maybe a Stanley knife, butcher's knife, a saw, anything in fact which may have been used. The Civilian searchers and the Coastguards will now be stood down immediately as we search for Evans. We have no idea if he is armed, I'm not willing to put them at risk. I'll talk to the armed response chief, and we can formulate a plan of action."

Rogers agreed that she should return to the POLSAR search coordinator with the new development and promptly advise him to stand all non-police down. This was yet again developing into a long difficult task not even mentioning a dangerous one. She felt drained, realising she had not eaten for a number of hours, however she was pleasantly surprised to find that a welfare trailer had been provided by the locally based search team to provide its members with refreshments. She would see to it that her police colleagues were also cared for.

Keen to pass on the direction to stand down the teams, her own sandwich and a hot cup of tea would have to wait a while. The relevant information was passed on. Huws had also phoned in. The emphasis of the search now considerably changed with a significant potential risk to the public too. They needed to get Evans under lock and key sharpish.

Rogers realised that this smacked a little of a repeat of the Littleton case not too long ago, he had basically got away with only pleading guilty to the death of their police colleague Steffan Parry and totally avoided having four other deaths pinned onto him.

Search team members were gathering around the rendezvous point again now, a colourful bunch in their variety of protective clothing, demonstrating a varied level of energy. Some clearly having traipsed through dense undergrowth, up to their mid thighs in bracken, gorse and heather, boots and the trouser hems clinging muddied and wet to fatigued legs. A few, still with enthusiasm in their step having been allocated the easier task of the roadside verges and field edges.

Some were attempting to sidle across to the refreshment trailer but were stopped in their tracks by the leader of the Police search team, every other service giving abeyance to the superior authority in this instance. None of the civilian operatives wanted to appear subversive.

General Inter service chatter broke out at the news they were being stood down. Some by their fatigued state, pleased, others feeling distinctly that it was an incomplete task but appreciating that it was now a matter of preserving people's safety.

Within minutes the refreshment trailer was inundated with requests for tea and bacon butties. Rogers stepped in at this juncture and asked please would they mind if the police searchers could get first dabs, it was a certainty that they would be searching for many more hours. Once refreshed and fed, the police officers would be re briefed as to their next task.

Rogers made her way back to her car, keen to join up with Howard and Edwards and check her colleague was OK, as well as whether there had been any luck with finding any evidence on the implements. They had both however by now left with the new evidence for Bangor.

Chapter Twenty-Nine

THE SCRUFFY BULK of William Evans could well have been spotted if anyone was eagle-eyed enough to have glimpsed him outside the cottage, less than half a mile from where all the police were gathering on the edge of the common, an overgrown spindle of a Red Robin shrub more than likely disguising the contours of his body and casting an invisibility cloak of shadow over him. He knew it was silly to stay where he was, but he knew the fields well. He had made the decision when he had awoken from a nap in the relative comfort of the summer house. He knew that currently most of the searchers were collected around some sort of trailer and some were indeed leaving in singles and pairs in vehicles. He reckoned he would have maybe a good twenty minutes if he was quick about it, to make his way down across the fields back down towards the quarry.

He hoped that he had been successful in pushing the body of his victim over the cliff into the sea, to hopefully be picked over by the crabs and other sea creatures. The other man had got away from him but not until he had made a good job of injuring him. He had made off across the field towards the village less than half a mile away if he followed the path.

The fact that the policemen that morning wanted to search his sheds for the pitchfork he had carefully buried and burnt, might signify that the second man had been found.

He had let him go after a short stumbling chase on his part in order to take his spoils home. The rucksack left behind had been ideal to do this. That had then been stuffed into the top of the corn crusher. Unlikely anyone would find it there.

The old barracks shed would provide him with shelter for the night, then if he could get to the top of the old fort above the quarry the following day he may spot the searchers. His plan was to sneak around behind them and get back to his own home having made sure that they had left the premises.

All of this had been worked out in his head as a simplistic plan, no detail, assuming that he could outsmart tens of team members. He could only hope. He found himself hungry again.

Chapter Thirty

HUWS'S PHONE rang in his pocket. He was at that point, standing in a shed at Evans's farm alongside a team of officers who were literally taking the place apart. It was a den of antiquity. Some of the tools and equipment they were surrounded by had been there and well-used no doubt, for generations, a collection of pale brown hessian sacks which had their own unique smell of ancient rodent impregnated dust, gathered in the weave for decades. The sheds contained everything and anything from wooden drain rods which Huws knew as a certainty having been inside the house that they had not been used in any way shape or form in recent times.

Gate hooks and hangers, ball cocks no doubt for the water troughs, heat lamps, bulb less, and webbed with ancient cobwebs that would have warmed many a lamb or litter of piglets.

Can upon can of oil, for tractors, some unopened, some empty, likely drained out of various sumps in buckets, the body of an unfortunate long-dead rat skimmed in black oil almost preserved in its slimy grave.

The team worked their way religiously through the sheds working right to left.

Huws answered the phone. DS Howards name on the screen.

"Any luck?" he asked hopefully. "Found anything useful? Nothing much of any use here so far, but we have two, well one and a half more sheds to go through."

Huws paused long enough that Howard was able to get a word in.

"Yes Sir, they have done a few tests on both the remnants of the wooden handle and the metalwork. Blood traces on both, Luminol showed blood straight away on the handle, the metalwork needs more tests. It was more difficult to differentiate on the iron fork as Luminol will show up as luminescence on iron, but there are enough traces on the wood to provide samples despite him trying to burn it.

They got a decent enough trace to prove transfer of blood quite possibly from the victim's hand where he may well, or likely both of them tried to fight off the attacker, or as also believed, in the attempt to even pull the pitchfork out of their abdomen. The whole picture is horrific. We are looking to match the blood of both victims to the blood on the handle.

They seem confident they'll get good fingerprints from the handle of the attacker and his victim's; I presume the forensics officer at your end is able to get plenty of fingerprints in the house that belong to Evans? Obviously, to be totally conclusive we will need some prints from the man himself.

There are further chemical tests that they just need to do on the metalwork to prove that the reactants are actually showing blood and not just reacting to the iron itself."

He repeated this point, already mentioned as if seeking to emphasise that he had indeed taken in all that had been said, especially after his earlier display of what he chose to call weakness.

"Good, good, we no doubt have him don't we? If we could only find the bugger," said Huws.

"Well hopefully yes, there will be plenty of evidence to put him away. The team here in Bangor say that they will have a look at the pathology report from Dr Emyr Rowlands to compare the detail on the stab injuries with the size of the pitchfork now we have it in our possession."

"Well done lad. I'm going to stay here for a while, I'm sure they won't take much longer now to go through the last couple of sheds, then we will be done here though I plan to leave a car down here with a couple of officers in it, just in case boyo has any plans on coming back home.

Yourself, Edwards and Rogers better get off home for a few hours kip, who knows what we will have ahead of us tomorrow. I'll catch up with Rogers and tell her shortly."

"Right Sir, if you're sure, but I'll be at the end of the phone if you want me, don't hesitate to ring. I'll pass the message on to the other two. Griff is here in the car with me now but Rogers I think has gone back to the station."

"Yes, she was going to organize some food for our search officers; she must have got that sorted and then left."

Chapter Thirty-One

EVANS KEPT an eye on the search party in the fields below, they were still searching the field edges and painstakingly going through a small woodland to his far-right. He chose his moment carefully when most had their backs to his current position and keeping himself low he followed the boundary wall along the field to his left and made his way down the narrow lane. This, if he continued would bring him down to the beach below, but he would nip through a gate to his right soon and follow the field edge down to the old footpath which was now largely replaced by the new coastal path route. On reaching the old path he had to struggle to climb an old gate, this would bring him towards the edge of the cliff to the path the old quarrymen would have used daily. Long disused and not just a tad dangerous.

Soon he could see the quarry ahead and down below to his left, he paused to catch his breath. Advancing age had certainly taken its toll on his health. The track from here was now overgrown with bracken which was just taking on a spring greenness. Thick rope-like old heather caught his feet as he tried to keep to the remnants of the path. To fall now and hurt himself would be a disaster. It wasn't as if he was just a random coastal walker, injured and calling for help. The path down to the beach zigzagged down the cliff face, old work boots over the years, having long abandoned their daily slog. His feet slid from under him causing him to flail at the heather, breaking his slide, but not to be relied on for purchase so fragile were the roots on the rock face.

He eventually reached the pebbly beach down below, and half walked, half clambered as the stones slid under his weight down the steep shore into the sea. He knew there was a fair depth of water here, hence why there had at one time been a pier. To slide down and into the water, would be the end of him. Growing up in a beachside village induced a sense of respect in its children, the sea not to be taken lightly. He had no memory ever of having been taught to swim as a child and now was not the time to learn.

The gaping mouth of the empty sheds were to his right, red rusted metal girders twisted and bent, this was where he executed his first deed. He walked past as quickly as his tired feet would take him, unwilling to re conjure the images in his mind's eye.

A dash of colour caught his eye from above, a strip of blue and white tape still attached to a wooden post on the track edge above. He paused to listen to any sounds from above, aware that his own footsteps on the crunching pebbles would no doubt have alerted anyone that may be up there already.

He continued with caution, his breath coming in irregular gasps between pauses of trying to hold his breath and at the same time remain silent. He started climbing the steep slope to the middle level. Halfway up he paused and looked along the cliff ledges ahead of him, hoping that there would be no evidence of the carcass that he pushed over the edge. Using the word carcass made it easier for him to accept, denoting more the idea that it could have been an animal that he had skilfully butchered.

Nothing could be seen, he comforted himself with the thought that the remains would no doubt be at the bottom of the sea, and every day as the ligaments broke up would look less and less like a human skeleton as it was pounded by the waves against the foot of the cliffs.

He trudged on cautiously around the hairpin at the top of the slope where a turning space had been created. He had no idea why that would have been done. To be seen on his left now was the old barracks, other than a few gaping holes in the roof, it would still provide him with shelter.

Shocking him to his core he saw that the building was surrounded by blue and white police tape, he shook his head to no one other than himself, there was no one here, but it was very obvious to him that there had been and very recently. Had the real depth of his evil deed been discovered? Had the young man actually got away alive and reported his ordeal? His mind was racing, should he stay here, would the police be back, or had they completed their investigations here? How much did the police know?

He kicked himself for his stupidity. Had he just let the police look around his sheds they would have found nothing more than the day they came looking for his son and the rewards of his drug running.

He was not in the least bit perturbed that they had found and removed the drugs haul, he had no interest in those. He had no idea whatsoever what to do with them.

What would he do now? He was exhausted, there wasn't much more moving in him this evening. The day was closing in now, still early spring.

He chose to enter the barracks and find himself a corner to sit and rest. His appearance in a smaller back room caused the sudden exit of a surprised rat. He was well-used to their company, he had no fear of them, unlike his own mother who was petrified. He made himself as comfortable as he could, hoping the night would not be too cold.

He fell into a fitful disturbed sleep having decided he would keep to his plan and cautiously move on to the top of the old fort which was not far. From there he could tuck himself away amongst the rocks and watch the world go by below. Most importantly he may be able to see the police search party and make his way around them and back to his home. Surely they would have finished their search there and found nothing of importance to them.

As he slept, the ousted rat returned, unbeknown to the sleeping man it curled up in the crook of his knees and enjoyed the warmth of the human body until the sun rose. The light shining in through the glassless window shone directly onto the dishevelled heap, making him twitch and mutter in his pre waking moments. The rat scuttled away to get on with its daily business.

Chapter Thirty-Two

EDWARDS APPEARED in the office and sat down opposite Rogers; she had a large mug of coffee in front of her.

"Make me a coffee will you? If the kettle's already boiled?" asked Edwards.

The stare she returned would have turned hell to ice.

"Since when have I been your skivvy?"

"Sorry, do you want another one? I see by the skin forming on that one that it will have been yesterdays. What are you tapping away at?" Edwards attempted to cover up his faux pas.

"I'm writing up the report of yesterday's search results, God knows why I'm bothering because absolutely nothing has been found. The teams took a break between 2am and 7am and are, as we speak, awaiting further orders today. They will use the drone again today and the police dog team when it's available. The area Search and Rescue dog team coordinator did offer to get a few dogs together, but we decided that as we were not looking for a 'normal' missing person we didn't want to put their handlers at risk."

"So, it is a waiting game again."

She continued, "The DI stayed at the farm until all the sheds had been checked over and nothing significant was found that would help us with our case, the other sheds were just full of general detritus and the old freezer where Ashley Williams had stashed his drugs haul in that drug trafficking case."

Edwards nodded.

"Heard or seen Justin this morning? He was in a bad way yesterday when we were locked in that shed. We really should try to persuade him to get some help. You know don't you, that he has not really given himself any time to grieve after he lost Steff, sad enough, that they had kept their relationship a secret, but he took no time off at all, just ploughed on to get the Littleton bloke behind bars, but you know full well like I do, that he is still beavering away trying to get enough evidence together to pin the other four on him too."

Rogers shook her head.

"I've not seen him since yesterday, I won't phone him yet, he will accuse me of nagging him. Maybe he has spoken to the DI already, he will tell us when he gets in. I think the DI just wants to get our team together this morning, so we can confirm what has been done to date, so we are all singing off the same hymn sheet."

Edwards nodded and grabbed his mug off his desk and picked up Rogers's mug for a refill. Returning with two full mugs.

"I've just been thinking, this bloke, Evans, if we think he is responsible for the murder of two men, one who had by all accounts been stripped of most of his flesh?"

Rogers, raising her gaze from her screen, looked Edwards in the eye. She stood up with such force that her chair fell behind her with a metallic clatter.

"Jesus Christ, the freezer in his shed, what hell sort of meat is he storing in there?"

Edwards was still holding both mugs of coffee as Rogers speed-dialed their boss. His jaw once again hung open in full recognition of what his colleague was inferring.

"Sir, Boss, uhm, where are you right now?" she asked, almost demanded.

She nodded in response to whatever the answer was.

"OK we will both meet you there, we will defer the team

meeting until we know more, Oh, before you hang up, have you heard from the DS this morning? He hasn't turned up yet, I thought he may have phoned you."

She looked up at Edwards, and continued.

"He had a bit of a turn yesterday in the barn, a bit of a panic attack, Griff and I are worried about his state of mind, can you ring him? He may well be less annoyed at you contacting him than if we do it?"

The answer had been in the affirmative. Rogers closed down the screen of her computer and grabbed her coat off the back of the chair. She grabbed her coffee from Edwards's hands and declared, "You can drive, did you bring a biscuit?"

Chapter Thirty-Three

EDWARDS AND ROGERS sped down the farm track as quickly as the potholes allowed, DI Huws already there, confirmed by the presence of his car.

Edwards was still putting the car in neutral and pulling on the handbrake when Rogers jumped out and started striding off towards Huws.

"Which shed is the freezer in?" She demanded a little curtly thought Edwards, after all, she was aiming this at their DI. He took no umbrage and walked with her towards the left-hand shed.

"In here, the lads have looked all around the shed and just lifted the lid which basically confirmed that the old boy just keeps his food in here. It works off a genny which he obviously keeps going." Huws was passing on information that he had been told.

"But is there anything else in the freezer? You know like other food, the sort that other people might store in there. Bags of frozen peas, maybe a couple of emergency loaves of bread, some frozen roast potatoes, anything other than meat?"

"I have to admit I haven't looked myself, thinking about it now it seems so bloody obvious."

Huws was annoyed with himself for just not looking at the

bigger picture. It was all well and good looking for weapons, but....he shook his head at his stupidity.

Edwards was looking around the shed in general whilst Rogers and Huws made towards the freezer on the back wall, both donning gloves. His attention had been taken by the old Lister grain crusher in the corner. There would have been a grain store above at one time, evident by the trap door in the low ceiling above his head. Grain would have been shovelled down into the chute, crushed and bagged into sacks below. His fascination with vintage machinery even now taking his attention.

"Has anyone had a look up above?" he asked. "I'm assuming no one has, as the cobwebs have not been disturbed."

"I wasn't aware of an upstairs." admitted Huws.

"Well, no, I doubt anyone would have considered looking up in the semi-dark with no proper lights, it only took my attention because I collect old machinery. Shall I see if there is anything that I can use to get up there?"

Edwards was off on the hunt before Huws had a chance to agree with his plan. Rogers however was now opening the hasp and staple home-made closure devise on the freezer.

She lifted the rusting lid with an effort, the rubber seal having perished and therefore making the electrics work far harder than necessary to keep the temperature down. The icy seal almost popped in the reluctant release of its lid. The freezer was half full. Plastic bags of every variety piled atop each other in a disorganized mess. This in itself disturbed Rogers's, her OCD with regards to her own freezer organization at home causing her to suck in a breath.

"Nothing labelled, just all piled in, how the hell does he know what he is going to be eating for his supper? Beef, lamb or pork, it could be anything. I'm sure most of it will be well past its use-by date too."

"Use by date?" asked Huws, astonished at her statement. "But it's in a freezer, surely it will last forever?"

The incredulous look that Rogers gave him, indicated it was certainly not the case.

"I'm surprised you haven't poisoned yourself Sir if you never check dates on your freezer contents."

He thought to himself that it had always been Gwen's job to manage such things, then his mother's when she invited herself to live with him during the Coronavirus lockdown. He made a mental note to himself to check the deep dark depths of his chest freezer in the garage when an opportunity arose.

Rogers was just starting to remove the top layer when Edwards returned with an old wooden ladder.

"I think this should take my weight so I can open the trap door and have a look up there."

"Well be careful, from what I can see there is more woodworm hole than ladder there."

Huws was pleased that the younger more agile Edwards was willing to risk his legs on climbing up.

"It's not too high Sir, just a little too far to pull myself up from the ground."

He had placed the ladder on the wooden framework at the edge of the trap door. Two rungs up allowed him to pop the wooden door onto its one-hinged side.

"Nothing to see, other than pigeon and mouse droppings-Oh! Hang on, I can see something green just showing at the entrance of the grain chute, I might actually be able to reach it if I just go up a couple more rungs."

Edwards was pushing himself up, Huws, made him hesitate.

"Do you have gloves on? Apart from handling potential evidence, I don't want one of my officers going down with Leptospirosis from the rodent pee, that happened to an old friend of mine years ago, he was proper poorly."

Edwards nodded in the affirmative and continued to stretch towards his target.

"There's a lot of grunting going on up there, hope the ceiling isn't going to come down on us both."

Huws was piggy in the middle now between two officers, holding the bottom of a ladder for Edwards and watching Rogers empty the very bowels of the freezer. Bag upon bag of meat growing now at Huws's feet. Well, he assumed it could be meat, the bags were so coated with frost, they could just as easily have been bags of rocks.

"How many more are there?" he asked.

Rogers was bent over to the point that he worried she would disappear totally out of sight into the icy depths.

"Only a couple more bags now, but they're stuck to the sides, won't be a moment. Two minutes."

Huws could hear Edwards grunting above their heads somewhere, a dragging sound of something being pulled across the floor above.

"Bingo," called Edwards.

"I've found a rucksack; it was stuffed down into the grain chute. Can I pass it down to you? Watch out for dust in your eyes, it's filthy up here. I haven't looked inside it yet, but there's something in it. I doubt that the old fella would have a use for a quality rucksack like this, doesn't look the hiking type to me."

Huws reached up to take the rucksack from above, Edwards followed on, not bothering to close the trapdoor after his feet touched the floor.

"Shall we have a look inside?" he asked his superior.

Edwards was already opening the clip fasteners and undoing the laced drawstring that drew the mouth of the rucksack closed. He looked into the depths before inviting Huws to do the same.

Lying at the bottom were at least two butchers knives and even a cleaver. Dried blood encrusting the dull steel of the tools in clotted smears. No effort whatsoever had been made to clean them. There was no doubt as to what these would have been used for.

"Don't pull the knives out Edwards, we will just get the bag as it is to the forensics lab later, but good spot," He paused, "even if you were only checking out farm machinery."

"Right, Sir, can we get back to the job in hand now?" demanded Rogers. "Can we have a look in one of these bags? My hands are bloody freezing after pulling all this out while Edwards plays at being Tarzan."

She started to attempt to tear the plastic covering off the first package, her senior officer merely stood and watched.

"Bit like Christmas this, you have no idea what is under the wrapping," added Edwards into the conversation.

"Uhm, do cows or pigs have tattoos on them?" asked Rogers whilst at the same time pushing the partly opened package away from herself in disgust.

"OK, OK, just stop now." Huws held his hands up.

"I think we all know what we're looking at here. I'll call the forensics department and tell them of our potential find and ask how they want to take it from here. In fact, I think we should repack the freezer as near as we can to how we found it. Then the oldest meat will be at the bottom again. I have a very bad feeling that the bag we have just opened may well be a body part from our first quarry victim."

"The skeleton?" gasped Rogers.

"Yes, I'm afraid so, and it was right under our noses all this time."

Edwards took no further part in the discussion, instead bolting outside just in time before he began retching.

Chapter Thirty-Four

JUSTIN HOWARD, pulled the quilt tighter around his shoulders, turning onto his side, grasping at the remnants of sleep that was leaving him. He had no idea what time it was and in all honesty, he didn't care. He had been late to bed, and once he couldn't put it off any longer, he replayed a film inside his head in glorious technicolour of what had happened to him earlier today.

It would probably not be a big thing at all to anyone else on the team, they would have laughed it off, but these past few months he had felt brittle, to the point of breaking. It was easier to just do the framework of his job and shut all the rest of his life out.

Justin felt he was living a false life, he felt the loss of Steff as if it had been yesterday, but time had gone by now to the extent that his colleagues never mentioned him, ever. It was as if he had never existed. He understood that they probably didn't want to rake up the feelings, little did they know that the volcanic eruption of stifled, no strangulated grief, bubbled between his guts and his throat. He knew damned well that if he allowed it the freedom to escape its repression, that he would not be able to control it and would be overcome with the pain of it.

For months, he had felt in control, being able to disguise his true feelings during his long hours at work, and like an addict going over and over Littleton's case in his free time to search for any tiny bit of evidence that they had overlooked.

There was never any. His files and notebooks, lay abandoned and on occasion thrown across the flat in fits of rage and desperation.

His sleep even was haunted by the case, nightmares, daymares, was there such a thing? His head was stuffed full of detail, detail, detail, it would not leave him alone, pecking at his brain day in day out.

He couldn't continue like that anymore.

The sunlight, seeping in around the edge of the blinds told him it was daytime, the sounds of traffic outside also indicating that it was not early-people were getting on with their daily lives. He would get up soon and shower. The thought of this in itself was too much of an effort. He had not had a proper shower for, too long to count. He put water over his hair which was in dire need of a cut and was heavy-handed with the aftershave. He was at least shaving when he could be bothered. He thought last night that he should put a wash on, the mountain of clothes in various piles around the bedroom and bathroom grew daily. He had in fact already delved into Steff's sock drawer when he had used up all of his own.

His phone had rung a couple of times that morning, it was in the lounge, probably on the settee where he had lain until the early hours. An empty bottle of wine would still be on the coffee table alongside another still half full.

He sat up, swinging his legs over the side of his bed, pushing the uncovered duvet aside, its cover in the wash basket weeks ago, still unwashed. He just couldn't be bothered. He walked across to the bathroom, looking across at his gaunt pasty face as he peed. Steff would be furious to see him like this. But who cared now?

Putting on the dressing gown that was hanging over the side of the bath, he made for the kitchen, a quick diversion into the lounge to pick up the wine bottle. He drank straight from the bottle as he put some bread in the toaster. Hair of the dog and all that.

Throwing the now-empty bottle into the overflowing bin he forgot his toast and sat at the breakfast bar, head in hands.

For the first time in months Justin wept, he wept the anguished despair that had been bottled up in him for months, he gasped for breath, mucus and tears ran down his face in equal measure, the cork was out of the bottle there was no stopping it.

His phone was ringing again in the lounge, nothing mattered to him now, he would not have cared if he died that very minute. He felt futureless, a dark void opening up in front of him, a great wall to be climbed that he had no particular desire to attempt. The random packets of Paracetamol, Ibuprofen, Co-codamol and, for some past reason that must have befallen one of them, the remains of a packet of Imodium, stared up at him from the cluttered coffee table, shouting at him persistently to 'Take us'. He was sorely tempted to look for the peace they would bring.

Chapter Thirty-Five

EVANS WOKE SLOWLY from his fitful slumbers, cold in the early spring dawn. Cold to his bones, a saying his old father used to use as he encouraged his son to put more coals on the fire. The birds were singing but having never been a nature lover, he had no recognition of the sounds, of which bird was which.

He stretched his legs out, stiff and sore after the extra exercise he had created for himself yesterday, added to this an increasing stiffness that his advancing age had bought to his knees and hips. He rolled himself over then raising himself firstly onto all fours he laboriously stood up, using the frame of the glassless window to help himself up. A careful look around to see how the land lay was needed to help him decide on a plan for the day.

Tiredness and hunger had dissipated his enthusiasm somewhat for a life on the run, but what choice did he have.

If it was quiet all around he would make his way onto the top of Arthur's table, the fort, and see what he could see.

He decided it was safe enough for him to leave the building, he would take his time walking the zigzag track up the hill to the gateway, just cautious in case there were still any police officers around.

It was quiet, only the cries of the gulls wheeling overhead to be heard, above the odd bleat of an early lamb that had lost sight of its mother, stupid creatures sheep, well in his opinion at least.

He walked diagonally across the field towards the flat-topped Fort. He used to play atop this as a young boy, together with the neighbouring farmers son's, not even knowing that it was any sort of ancient monument. To them, it was a castle from where they could fend off marauders- boys of his age from the nearby hamlet. They used to build dens from anything they could get their hands on, sheets of corrugated iron placed in gapped walls to fill the hole, discarded gates, that needed four gang members to carry from wherever it had been removed, Fronds of bracken, and clumps of gorse forming quick to collapse roofs. He allowed himself a smile at these memories, certain that should he have a good look around the eastern edge of the fort he might still find some of these discarded gates abandoned and overgrown by vegetation.

He arrived eventually at the edge of the flat plateau, no one to see. He had a 360-degree view, across the open sea, which on a clear day would expose the hills on the Isle of Man, and to the Northeast, The Cumbrian fells, both places he had never visited, never having had much interest in moving from his own square mile. To his west was the remainder of Anglesey and further round were the hills of Snowdonia on the mainland. At this point in his surveying, the thought struck him that he may indeed not see this again if he allowed himself to be caught.

A small part of his thoughts imagined that he may well be better off in prison where he would at least be cared for, fed, and warm. Was he ready to give up his freedom quite yet though?

Chapter Thirty-Six

GRIFF EDWARDS HAD DRAWN the short straw, having been told by Huws to wait at the farm for the forensic team to arrive. Two officers were actually sat at the end of the farm track, just on the off chance that their fugitive would chance to make his way home.

The search team would right now be starting on a thorough search. They had issued a press release early that morning asking people to keep a lookout for him. A brief description. Always a difficult thing to do in such a way that it made locals aware of the situation but not frighten them to death. He could after all be armed, he wasn't afraid to kill obviously.

'We are seeking the whereabouts of William Evans who is actively evading the police. We are hoping that no one is aiding him in his attempts to evade the police. Do not approach if seen, contact us via our webchat, or via Crimestoppers.'

Edwards found himself feeling anxious as he sat there in the yard, even though he was in his car, who knew how psychopaths like this worked?

He kept his eyes open and was pleased to see a van appear in his rear-view mirror. He waited for it to pull up next to him and disgorge two white coveralled personnel from the passenger side. Forensics.

They had obviously hired some sort of refrigerated van to transfer the contents of the freezer away back to the lab at Bangor.

The driver opened the two rear doors of the van, it had racks of shelving down both sides, he stood waiting expectantly, drawing on a vape which he had pulled out of his jacket pocket. He leaned on the van, one leg bent back in a casual pose, resting on a tyre.

"Hi," he acknowledged Edwards.

Edwards nodded in return.

"What's in the shed that needs a refrigerated van?" he asked.

"Nothing you need to concern yourself with son."

"Mm, my boss said I needed to keep my trap shut if he paid me to drive."

The two forensic officers were soon reappearing with bags of frozen meat, all now clearly tagged and labelled with numbers. They placed each bag meticulously in order in the van. None of the bags had been opened at this stage.

Edwards was hoping that the bags would not all be allowed to defrost at once, no doubt they would have their own plans to do this in the least unpleasant way for all concerned.

In the meantime, Rogers had accompanied Huws to the forensics lab to deliver the rucksack and its contents, the first rucksack that had been discovered in the initial search on the common had been proved to have no link whatsoever to their victims, it had for whatever reason simply been discarded.

The door buzzer rang with the voice of Huws's new 'friend' Greta Wilson, he was quite embarrassed at the idea of meeting her again, however knowing two of her staff were going to be at the farm, it was almost inevitable that she should be the one to let them in.

Rogers handed over the bagged rucksack, Wilson checked the tag and entered the details on the computer.

All the evidence so far clearly logged, timed and dated and any test results where relevant.

Rogers would have been quite interested to have a longer look at the work that had been done, though most of the tests were way over her head where chemicals were concerned.

The bag was carefully opened, the rucksack gently taken out. Rogers was itching to see what was inside.

She had to wait; Wilson took photos of it at every angle.

"I'll get prints off this. Is it likely we may have prints on it from multiple persons?"

"Well, yes, Edwards pulled it out of the corn crusher, but he had gloves on, but likely the murderer and one or both victims, we are unsure which of them it belonged to."

Wilson looked at Huws, he glasses dropped down onto the tip of her nose.

"OK, let's have a look at what is inside it then."

This was the moment Rogers was looking forward to, did they finally have their murder weapon?

Wilson carefully drew out the first knife, a broad-bladed knife, wooden-handled, clear handprints from a bloodied grasp, the stain-less-steel blade marked to the hilt with browning blood.

The second instrument was not a knife at all, handled with a grip similar to a hacksaw, it had a sharp serration to its blade, more akin to a saw. Liberally covered with blood.

The third instrument was a cleaver, cleaner, maybe not the instrument of choice in this case.

At the very bottom of the sack almost hidden in the lining was a knife, that had more similarity to a scalpel.

"I suspect this will have been used to separate the internal organs from their positions, the spleen, kidneys, and liver," offered Wilson.

"The knife will have been used to strip off the flesh and the saw to cut through the ribcage to access the heart from within. Obviously I need to discuss this in more detail with our friend Emyr Rowlands, so we can compare the instruments with the wounds inflicted."

The reality of the picture she was now posting in Rogers brain, would she imagined, be there forever. She felt shaky if she thought about the vision too much, slightly sick. She stood next to her DI making every effort to take some good deep breaths but with great efforts to hide her distress.

Wilson took a step towards her, pulling a wheeled lab stool along with her.

"Here, sit down before you fall down, you're almost see-through."

Rogers was pleased to take the seat, but also embarrassed.

"I'm OK Sir, really."

She looked across at DI Huws. His colour was not particularly great either.

Chapter Thirty-Seven

ROGERS AND HUWS sat silently in the car outside the Forensics department, watching the world go by. Not a word uttered, staring blankly through the breath misted windscreen. University students strolling by, ear pods and in the main scruffy. The world at their feet if they chose to put their noses to the grindstone and study.

Rogers phone beeped, she glanced at the screen -Edwards- Huws looked across.

"Anything of interest?"

She opened the text. "Ring me, developments."

She must have stared at the screen for too long causing her superior to give her a nudge.

"Go on then, ring him, we need every development we get, good or bad in this case, see what it is."

She pressed her keypad, none of them having a clue on individual numbers, just contact names or in many cases in their jobs, Nick-names.

"What's up?"

A long pause, lots of nodding.

"What is it?"

Demanded Huws by her side. She ignored his intrusion, continuing to listen.

"Mm. Wow. Really? When did you hear this? I can't believe it. Have you let Justin know about this? Oh, I'll try him as well then. He should be over the moon, if nothing else it will bring him closure. He hasn't stopped beavering away at that case. This will bring an end to it."

"Hey, what is it?" demanded Huws again.

"Tell you in a second, I just need to try to get hold of Justin, but its good news, Littleton has spilled."

"Good God, yes, tell him right away, is he not in the incident room?"

"No, not shown up today yet, Griff can't get him on the phone either. Probably had a rough night after his upset yesterday, wanting to compose himself maybe. You know how much he hates showing his feelings or as he described them to me once- his weaknesses. I did tell him that we didn't think that of him in any way, shape or form."

Rogers turned the phone screen to face her, double-checking she had the right number, she returned the phone to her ear.

"He isn't answering, I'll send him a text and a WhatsApp message. If he doesn't respond to those, I think I'll drive over to his house later."

Huws started the engine and pulled out onto the road, he nosed into the entrance of the car park opposite and turned around for their return journey.

The local city, which was Bangor, was busy, it would soon be the Easter break, but it was good to see the student population back again, giving some life and vibrancy to the place, it had been deathly quiet during Covid, barely anyone to be seen on the high street, not that he was a regular visitor other than his visit to the optician to update his prescription. It must have been a sign of getting older when they had offered him a free hearing test too.

The drive back to Llangefni was quiet from the traffic point of view, heading over the bridge and through Menai Bridge, Huws told Rogers to take the back road through Penmynydd back to the county town of Llangefni. It gave them a little headspace to absorb what they had learned at the Lab.

Huws had been invited for supper by Jane after work if timing allowed. He had not seen much of her over the last week with this case in full swing. Of course, they had spoken on the phone but things were still a little at arm's length in their relationship, nothing more than closeness on the sofa in front of the telly and the odd peck on the cheek.

Huws was pleased that he was not being pressurized to commit to a relationship as such at this stage and indeed he was sure that Jane felt the same. The fact that he had even voiced in his mind the word 'relationship' was a surprise to him. He smiled to himself.

They turned into the parking compound at Llangefni station, Rogers had glanced at her phone numerous times on the journey.

"No response from the DS?" asked Huws.

"No nothing, to be honest I'm getting a bit worried about him. It isn't really like him not to have his phone literally in his right hand all the time."

Huws was also worried, he had spoken to young Howard many a time in the months following Pc Steffan Parry's murder. Initially the young man had been open to conversation but recently he had become more and more closed off. Maybe he should have paid more attention to his obvious withdrawal, that was without the fact that he had become increasingly thin and gaunt. He understood from Howards' closest colleagues that he was spending all his free time trawling through the Littleton case, maybe now this would bring him closure and allow him to grieve.

Idris Huws was chewing these thoughts through, reminding himself firmly that he had no place to criticize Howard in any way shape or form.

Coming back to the present as he parked the car, turning to Rogers he began,

"Maybe you should have a chat with Griff Edwards and find out the details and log yourself a squad car and drive over to see what he is up to?"

"Yes please, thanks. I am worried about him, I think his panic attack at work yesterday was a huge thing for him. As soon as I've seen Griff, I'll drive over, I might even pop into Waitrose and get him something to eat, he is as thin as a rake these days, he needs to get a decent square meal inside him."

Huws made his way straight into his office, he needed to pass on the detail so far to DCI Williams, only then would he join them in the incident room to pass on the forensic lab findings, he expected the photos to have been sent shortly after he had left. He wanted to catch up with any search findings for Evans. At the end of the day, he would catch up with Rowlands, who would hopefully by then have been able to match up the weapons with the injuries on both young men, though the DNA would prove the connection anyway and Evans's prints would be all over them. All they really needed now was Evans himself.

Chapter Thirty-Eight

WILLIAM EVANS SAT on the edge of an ancient stone wall, no doubt once part of the defence mechanisms of the fortress. A brisk wind was blowing around him. He pulled his worn, greasy collar tighter around his neck. Looking across towards the mainland, the hills beyond the snaking route of the A55 road bringing traffic into North Wales. He couldn't claim to have travelled its route many times. He never, in the last couple of decades had much reason to leave his own island.

He had travelled the old road as a child, at least a couple of times during the summers, normally by bus, they weren't posh enough in those days to be called a coach, there was certainly no luxury involved. Sunday school trips either to Llandudno or Rhyl, Donkey rides on the beach, arcades, and fairground rides, the adults enjoying their time if anything, more than the children. The shackles of daily lives released for one long day. Laughing to the point where his mother and aunt literally wet themselves in the hall of mirrors, he had never seen his mother like that before.

. . .

These were usually trips organized by the Chapel, or Sunday school. Paid for with a weekly shilling into the kitty. This money was then used to collectively pay for the bus, and all the money over would have been divvied up between all the adults as spending money. This was to allow even the struggling families to have some fun and a bit of cash to pay their way.

Many a candy floss would have been eaten and in some cases vomited up in a bright pink burst over the seat back directly in front by the unfortunate child who could not cope with the twists and turns of the original road back along the coast to Anglesey. The only plus on the way back was the cheer and call to honk the horn as they drove through the tunnels through the headland rock faces. Hyms would have been sung loudly by all the devout passengers, many trying to make up for the fact that they had spent the afternoon in one of Rhyl's hostelries.

Many a parent, by the time they reached this part of the journey were pleased to see the Anglesey coast appearing to their right knowing they would soon be home and the excitement of the day would soon be forgotten in the hubbub of normal life.

Pulling the wing mirrors in, the bus driver would have to negotiate the narrow archways of the old chain bridge over the Menai Strait before then starting the job of dropping people off at various points near their homes, fathers carrying sleeping children, fraught bedraggled mothers carrying bags of coveted purchased goods that never looked as sparkling and necessary in the reality of home.

His mind was far away when he heard a shout from over his right shoulder. He struggled to his feet, ungainly and stiff, pulled up his overlarge new to him trousers and quietly and carefully made his way east over the brow of the hill, he would descend through the gorse and make his way down towards the old Church, he could sit quietly behind the building and think what his next move might be.

His enthusiasm for the life of a fugitive was however, already waning.

Chapter Thirty-Nine

DCI WILLIAMS HAD BEEN PLEASANTLY ACCEPTING of the news surrounding the progression of the case. Not his usual brusque dismissive self. Always concerned about costs.

The other topic of conversation was not only Williams's own imminent retirement but in fact Idris's own retirement from the job. This had been put off twice now due to the happenings on his patch in the last couple of years. Williams was looking forwards to endless days playing golf with his cronies, holidays away to Spain and Portugal, holidays where the men would play golf and the women would idle the days away chatting, gossiping about other police wives and drinking gallons of Prosecco by the pool.

It was not the type of retirement that Huws had envisaged for himself.

. . .

Most of his dreams for his future, however long he was blessed to have, had always involved his late wife Gwen, who would have dragged him away to various self-catering cottages in the Lakes or the Highlands, enjoying the scenery and long arduous walks. What would his retirement hold for him now? Would Jane be part of it?

Unlike a lot of people, police officers served for thirty years in service as a norm, unless they stayed on. He had never fancied the promotion to DCI, particularly if it was mainly office-based as Williams had chosen, anything for an easy life, ordering from on high.

No, he felt that he was still relatively young, young enough to enjoy his life, maybe even having a second career to boost his not too measly pension. It was something he needed to think about, once this case came to its conclusion. He still had his old mum to consider and Elin, living the high life at university, she still did not seem to have a definite plan for what she wanted to do. She was a bright young thing with a sensible head on her shoulders though and he doubted she would come home to live again, but instead get herself sorted with a flat or similar.

Williams had suggested that maybe they should have a joint retirement do somewhere.

Huws was not at all sure about that.

Chapter Forty

ROGERS PLACED the shopping bag in the passenger foot well, knowing full well that it was not really becoming of a police officer to visit a supermarket whilst on duty in a marked car. In all honesty, she didn't give a fig as she made her way to Justin's house. His car at least was outside. Dragging the bag with her out of the car, she strode up to the front door, a feeling of trepidation as to how she was going to deal with her upset colleague.

She rang the bell, followed by a rapid triple tap on the glass panel with her car key fob. No response. She rang again. Nothing. She pulled her mobile phone out of her vest pocket and dialled his number.

"Come on Jus, open the door."

She shouted through the letterbox, she could hear his phone ringing somewhere in the house. She tried his landline number. Same again, ringing but no answer.

She dropped her shopping at the door and made her way around towards the front of the house. She couldn't peek through the windows as was her plan, the blinds were pulled down.

"Justin, come on mate, you're worrying me now," she spoke purely to herself.

She scrolled the screen of her phone, this time choosing Griff's number. It was answered on a second ring.

"I'm at Justin's house. I'm worried, he isn't answering the phone, all the blinds downstairs are closed, so I can't see in. I've shouted through the letterbox, and he isn't answering. His car is here and so is his phone because I can hear it ringing in the house."

"OK, I will clear it with the Guv, and come over there to join you. I don't have a great feeling about this. He was in a hell of a state when we got shut in the barn. Shouldn't be long if Huws says OK."

Rogers picked up the bag of shopping and made her way back to the car. She may as well wait there. She rummaged through the bag and pulled out a posh packet of crisps. Justin wouldn't mind. She was, as per usual, starving.

The twenty minutes it took Griff Edwards to get to her felt like three hours. Her imagination was going wild. It struck her that maybe she should have phoned an ambulance, the thought that Justin had done something stupid rising to the forefront of her mind.

She leaped out of her car when Griff arrived.

"What the hell have you got there?" she shouted at him, knowing exactly what it was in his right hand, no answer needed. It was the Ram that they used on occasion to break down people's doors.

"We can't break his door down, can we?"

"You better believe it when I say, I will definitely be using this if he doesn't answer the door now. I reckon he's just closed himself in and got pissed."

Edwards did not sound totally convinced by his own ideas.

They both repeated the door knocking and shouting, giving their colleague time to realise that he might as well answer than ignore them any longer.

"Right, enough." Edwards went to make for the back of the house.

"We can't mess about any longer, I will get in through the back door, the DI said to do what I needed to get in if it came to it, come on."

Rogers followed close on his heels.

"He'll go mad if we smash his door."

"We can worry about that later. Do you have any other helpful suggestions?"

Edwards was already drawing the Ram back, feet apart to give himself a strong base, he swung, the door took three hard battering's, the lock finally giving way along with a splintering of the frame.

"Oh shit, he'll go mad."

Rogers was right behind Edwards as he pushed the door open, already shouting.

"Jus, mate, where are you?"

They half-ran through the back hall into the open-plan kitchen.

"Jeez, looks as if a bomb has dropped in here."

The worktops were strewn with packaging, dirty dishes, likely every mug Justin owned, empty or half full, coffee-stained rims. The kitchen table was covered with files and papers, lever arch boxes, documents. Waste paper basket tipped over, full of crumpled discarded sheets of scribble-covered papers.

Rogers was rooted in the centre of the room, not believing the mess her usually immaculate colleague had clearly created.

"That bloody Littleton man, all his fault."

"Get in here now."

Came a shout from another room, Edwards sounded frantic. Rogers sprinted through to a bedroom, equally untidy. Edwards was sitting on the bed, Justin, gripped in his hold, pale, lips showing a terrible blueness, spreading out towards his nose. Froth was running down his chin, head lolling. His bare upper body clammy and sweaty.

"He's alive- call an ambulance, he's barely hanging on."

Rachel Rogers was frozen to the spot, phone in hand, the usually totally calm person that normally lived inside her, gone somewhere. They could not lose another colleague.

"Rachel, phone, now!"

Edwards was lowering Justin onto the floor, carefully placing him on his side. He pulled the duvet off the nearby bed to hide his nakedness. He took care to avoid the stinking pool of vomit, that could be a good thing? He thought, not remembering any of his first aid training to be useful. Always easy when it was a stranger.

"Come on mate, hang on in there, we have Littleton, you know? He fessed up, for whatever reason, he's admitted to the other murders too. We've got him. You've got him, just hang on mate."

"I'll just go and open the front door for when the crew get here." Rogers seemed reluctant from sheer terror to stay in the room.

"Phone the Guv as well, he needs to know about this."

Rachel was glad of a job, she spoke to DI Huws, who had barely answered her, simply saying he would be as quick as he could. She forced herself back into the bedroom.

"Don't let him die," she pleaded.

"He is still breathing, but only just about, it's very slow and ragged, have a look around near us here and see if you can find what he might have taken, there are some packets on the other side of the bed on the floor."

Edwards had taken charge, recognising the panic that had overcome his colleague, realising she was millimetres from breaking down in tears. Something he well knew she would hate to do.

"Where the hell is the ambulance crew?"

Rogers was searching around on the floor collecting empty packets of tablets, paracetamol in the main, some Ibuprofen, Voltarol, Imigram, and Imodium. Quite a mixture of random stuff. All empty, but obviously they would have no idea how many were in the packets to start with. She heard the siren, threw the packets onto a bedside table and rushed to meet the crew. Huws was hot on their heels having returned from Bangor after a visit to see Emyr Rowlands.

The crew were efficient and tender in their handling of their friend, he was examined thoroughly, but the need to get him to the nearby hospital was classed as urgent. Huge difficulties in getting venous access were experienced, but as soon as the bag of fluid was connected. Edwards held the bag up, as the two crew members gently transferred Justin onto the carry chair. A decision was taken due to the corners and narrowness of the corridors. Edwards continued to hold the bag aloft, as he was further transferred onto the awaiting stretcher, a quick check of the drip delivery wheel by the paramedic and the bag was hung off the stand. Edwards and Rogers at this point left the ambulance, as Huws stepped up into the ambulance.

"I'm coming with you," he declared, a statement as opposed to a request. As a comment thrown into the wind he turned to the two anxious faces in front of him, "Not a word about this at the station, just think something up, don't lie, just be economical with the truth."

Rogers had put all the medication together in a carrier bag, she pushed it towards the paramedic closing the door, adding that he seemed to have potentially drunk a fair amount of alcohol too, though whether that was today or before, they didn't know.

Rogers and Edwards watched the ambulance pull away, lights and sirens, thankfully they were literally minutes from the hospital as long as the traffic was not too bad on the bridge.

Edwards put his arm around Rogers's shoulders, she seemed small as she moved closer to him, both drawing comfort in their shared distress.

Chapter Forty-One

WILLIAM EVANS WAS PLEASED the ancient old church had a Porch, quite a large one at that. He was disappointed however, that the door was locked. The solid stone bench along one side provided a perch to sit on at least, albeit a very cold. He could just about lie on it later on if he had to, provided he didn't move about too much.

He hadn't heard any more voices nearby and he suspected that they may not concentrate too near the quarry. They would already have covered that meticulously in the last couple of days.

He had wondered often to himself why he felt absolutely no guilt for what he had done. His Chapel upbringing and hours spent reluctantly at Sunday School should have taught him the error of his ways, but no, nothing.

As a young child, he was emotionally cold, towards his parents, school friends, even the odd pet that had been foisted upon him by well-meaning family members.

He had strangled his cat as a seven-year-old, no particular reason on the cat's part, but he had enjoyed the power it had given him. Burying it, he realised he hadn't even known its gender, it hadn't become a he or she, just a thing, buried deep within the stinking muck heap.

He did remember that he enjoyed digging it up a month or so later, to observe its decomposition.

He was a compulsive liar, even at that young age. Manipulating his few school friends in all sorts of ways, to his own benefit. This behaviour and attitude had caused them all to withdraw from him despite his mother inviting various children to tea after school. None of them ever turned up much to his mother's disappointment after her efforts at having prepared a sumptuous birthday tea.

Moving on to killing people had just seemed a small step up to him, he cared not of their value as a person, or their lives, families. He felt each was valid to satisfy his own needs and some people had just been in the wrong place at the right time from his point of view. He almost felt like it was his god given right.

Deep into his reflections, he laughed out loud at the fact that he had now ended up this very day taking shelter in a chapel. After childhood and his release from the control of his mother's apron strings he had not darkened the doors of a religious sanctuary until today.

He wondered what prison might be like, could it be that bad? Surely he would be fed, clothed, warm. This was better than he had currently. It may well be a good choice now as he was getting older.

It was pointless trying to make his way home again. Once they had discovered the contents of the freezer, the game was up anyway. Or was it?

A fair few body parts had been stored in the cold depths of that reliable old cold store. The more recent on the top. He should have been more organized and used the bottom layer first, but he had got lazy, the bottom layer had been there more years than he cared to remember now. He had no appetite for what lay down there in the depths at the bottom, in fact, he had never been able to bring himself to cook any of those portions. Part of him had been afraid he would somehow poison himself.

Most of the remains of his old sheepdog were in the bottom somewhere too, that had been a difficult eat, not so much because of liking the dog, but consequent to him rarely remembering to feed the animal, there had not been much meat on him.

They would no doubt have fun sorting all of that out.

The past looped in his mind as he settled down to lie on the stone slab, he would not stay here long. Awaiting darkness he decided he would after all make his way home, let himself in the back door if there was no one around, and sit and await his destiny.

Chapter Forty-Two

HUWS HAD SPENT a long night in resus, or as it was in reality, on a fake leather armchair in the relative's room next door. This had by its state, not been used much during Covid, no relatives allowed in and all that. More of a store room now for random medical bits and pieces. A kind nurse had at least bought him a blanket to keep him warm and a pillow for his head.

He could hear the sounds of monitors and voices all through the night and had popped out sporadically for any information or for a desperate pee, so worried was he of missing some critical activity or change in the young officer lying on the trolley behind the curtains. He was currently stable, blood tests, and every other conceivable test had been done. He was holding his own. The decision had been made early after his admission not to wash out his stomach contents, much which would no doubt have already gone, by the evidential presence of vomit. Quite likely with the passage of time the drugs would have been absorbed anyway. They chose to treat him symptomatically. The drug most concerning them apparently the Imodium tablets, causing his digestive system to slow its work dangerously and affecting his kidneys. Multi-organ failure had been pointed out as a real risk.

Critical but stable is what he told Edwards and Rogers when they had turned up at the hospital doors for news.

He had told them both to return home and get a good night's sleep. Evans was still on the run and had to be caught. They needed to be fresh in the morning. A fresh search team would be flooding the area. A real manhunt now. The greatest difficulty was keeping local residents at bay.

Chapter Forty-Three

EVANS STIRRED in his old armchair, rearranging the hessian sack makeshift pillow under his bottom as a spring poked up and annoyed him. He had used his mother's old dressing-gown to plump it up for a bit of comfort. He had crossed the fields in the early hours, carefully keeping his head down below the hedgerows, the back door was open, no one was around that he could see.

It was cold in the house, but he dared not light a fire, for fear of the smoke being seen from the closest neighbours who had no goodwill towards him, may well report their observations to the police.

He sat in his chair, slowly stiffening up as a result of his clambers around the countryside. He was getting older now, he would need to re-evaluate how he would live out his last years.

Chapter Forty-Four

A TIRED-LOOKING young Doctor entered Huws's room in the early dawn. Panicking initially, he stood up in expectation of bad news.

"Our patient is awake, he's not really responsive yet, but he is holding his own now and not needing oxygen. We'll however need to keep careful observations over the next couple of days, regarding his urine input and kidney function. He is still receiving fluid and his liver will be struggling too, trying to break down all the toxins, but we are hopeful we can support his organs sufficiently to pull him through this, especially considering he is otherwise a fit young man with no apparent co-morbidities. They'll transfer him to a private room up on the wards shortly, where he can be kept an eye on."

He paused and cleared his throat.

"Uhm, due to the fact that Mr. Howard attempted to take his own life, it is trust protocol for the mental Health team to have a chat with him. They can't do this for a couple of days due to time constraints, but that will at least give him a bit of time to recover."

Huws looking pained at this explanation.

"I would much rather that job was left to our own teams, it will be much better for him all around. We understand the job and its pressures. I'd like it kept in house. He will get the help he needs and as much time off to recover as necessary with limitless support."

"Are you sure? That's not our normal practice" The medic didn't sound convinced.

Huws nodded. This, as far as he was concerned, was best kept under the radar. If his superiors got to know, they may not be quite as committed as he and his team would be. He knew they would throw an invisible cloak of protection over their colleague and friend and nurse him back to full health and capacity. He was a good young detective with a sparkling future ahead of him.

Finding his phone in his back pocket, he rang Rogers.

"Yes, boss, how is he?" the phone had barely even rung. He knew they would be waiting for news.

"Looking very hopeful now. Not quite out of the woods yet, but they have told me I can pop through and see him for a chat before they move him to a ward upstairs. Once I'm happy to leave him, I'll be straight over."

"Mm, you may well be better popping to see Wilson in the Forensics lab. She phoned, wanting to speak with you. Refused to tell me what she wanted, but it's clearly about the freezer contents. My guess is they've been able to link the DNAs of the two lads and maybe the previous Misper."

Pushing the phone into his pocket he chose to go to see his young DS first, he always had his priorities right when it came to his team.

He hesitated behind the resus room curtains; he could hear the regular quiet breaths. It sounded a million times better than the gasps his young DS had been desperate for the previous evening. Pulling aside the curtains he stepped in. Justin Howard didn't stir. There was no chair next to him, just bleeping monitors, drip stands, blood pressure stands and various other monitoring paraphernalia, a soft plastic bag holding a small amount of overly dark urine hung off the side of his bed, the obvious catheter pipe disappearing under the light green blanket.

"Justin, can you hear me?" Huws almost whispering. "Justin lad, it's me, Idris."

Justin stirred, opened his darkened lids revealing bloodshot eyes. Small dark vessels spread over yellow whites. It shocked Idris Huws, though he tried to ignore it for the sake of the young man.

A single tear ran down Justin's cheek.

"I wanted to die. I didn't want this," His voice hoarse and rasping.

"I just miss Steffan so much, I'm useless by myself, I need him. Now likely I will lose my job as well and everyone will see how weak I am."

He stopped talking and slowly turned on his side away from Huws.

Huws walked around to face him.

"Justin, you will not lose your job. We will all look after you in the team, you can have as much time off as you need to get yourself better. We'll all pull together and get you some help. We don't need to let this get any further than our team."

Idris Huws sincerely hoped at this point that he could indeed keep his promise. He knew there was help within the force, there were even special places around the country that Justin could go to, however, he would be amongst strangers. Sometimes it was better to be amongst the people that had shared the good and bad with you.

This had indeed been the case for himself many moons ago after an incident. If it had not been for his friends, he would have jacked in the job there and then. God knows where he would have been by now.

Huws took hold of Justin's hand, clammy and slightly cold.

"Everything will be fine, you'll see. Maybe when you get better, I can take a bit of leave too, and we can have that Scottish walking holiday I talked about, beg a few Munro's before I get too old. I can show you a few spectacular spots in the Highlands that Gwen and I fell in love with years ago."

"I think I might like that."

Justin had a hint of a smile on his pale pink lips, he was falling asleep as he uttered the words.

A porter put his head around the curtain, they were ready to move him upstairs. Huws gave the young officer's hand a squeeze, which was just about reciprocated he said his goodbyes.

Happy that the outlook was not as bleak as it had been twelve hours or so ago. He left the hospital. Only then did he remember that he had no car.

No worries, worse things happened at sea. He would take a taxi into the city and see what Miss Greta Wilson had for him. It was pretty obvious that she had worked through the night.

His phone rang again before he had a chance to Google for a local taxi company. It was his friend Emyr Rowlands.

"Idris, it's Emyr, have you time now to put your head around the door of the path lab at the hospital? Greta Wilson had the contents of the freezer bought straight to me here. Not something I was exhilarated about because of the space, but she persuaded me to work through the night to see if we could piece these bodies together."

Just in time, before he took himself to the other end of the city for a wasted journey.

"I'm right outside, as it happens, had a couple of things to sort out. Five minutes I will be with you."

He had not mentioned Justin Howards' incident and suddenly he realised that he had not told the young officer that Littleton had coughed to all the murders. Mind you, he thought to himself, he needed to catch up with all those facts later in the office.

Chapter Forty-Five

BOTH ROGERS and Edwards had caught up with the POLSAR chief by phone, they were quite satisfied that they were perfectly in control of the search for Evans. Fresh team members had been bought in from outside the area. Still keeping clear of civilian search teams for this job due to unknowns around Evans being armed or not.

They had made the decision to pop around to Justin's home and at least make an effort to clean up the place before he came from the hospital. Rogers had armed herself with a bingbag, and a whole collection of cleaning materials. Edwards had been reluctant; Rogers persuasive skills had won him over. Rogers had also declared that she would bring her own bedding and set herself up on Justin's sofa so that he would not be alone when he eventually returned home.

Edwards had expressed his views on that. "I can't see Jus being very chuffed about that?"

"Tough." Had been her response.

"I can make sure that he has a few decent square meals inside him, just for the first week. His body will have taken a fair knock. I hope he hasn't caused himself any lifelong damage."

"Always the one for drama." laughed Edwards, pleased to be a tiny bit more optimistic about the well-being of their friend.

Huws by this time had spent an hour masked and gowned alongside a slightly truculent Rowlands. Normally easy-going, tiredness had brought a distinct grumpiness. Wilson however, despite not having been to bed at all was as cheery as she ever seemed, which was minimal.

Each bag of flesh had been carefully released from its plastic bag covering, and a hugely complex jigsaw of body parts was growing on the stainless-steel tables in front of them.

Nothing complete, random parts which had to be untied from their crude butcher's knots where Evans had attempted to create some shape to the hacked off pieces. Maybe in some sort of macabre effort to simulate a butcher's joint.

Huws was horrified to see not two possible people taking shape but at least four. Well, at least there were four tables covered with portions.

The fourth had bought gasps of shock from Jane who had turned up in the early hours to assist Rowlands, having been stood up by Huws, she joked with a wink. The fourth was much smaller, believed initially to be the remains of a child. Greta Wilson however after much examining had declared it could well be a skinned dog. This had almost horrified them more than the expected bodies at the realization of just how low this human being had stooped.

"We can hopefully now match at least two of the bodies with the victims, as in the young man we retrieved from the quarry a couple of days ago, and possibly the skeletal remains that were found on the beach will match up with what we know about that victim, the tattoo's etc. Animal DNA is different by about 1%, well that is my understanding of Chimpanzee DNA, dogs may have more variables. That will need more work, it doesn't quite look like lamb or beef, far more striated and leaner."

She continued to poke around amongst the pieces.

"Dog?" asked Rowlands. "I've not done an autopsy on a dog ever, doesn't come with the job, but could he have killed and skinned a dog?"

The silence in the room was tangible, the real horror of what they were witnessing right there in front of them on the table. The small crowd was almost holding their breath.

"The other body?" asked Huws, coming out of a dreamlike disbelieving state.

"Well, no way of knowing yet, but I will say that bar a small section of thigh, these tied portions here likely make up a whole body. I think it is certainly older, it has that look of a joint of beef that has been in the freezer for too long. We will need to do more tests on this to see if we can age it more accurately."

Wilson was moving the portions around like a giant puzzle as she spoke.

"I think this man is a dangerous psychopath that needs to be put away and before he strikes again. He certainly didn't just eat what he killed; he kiledl in order to maintain a guaranteed supply."

Chapter Forty-Six

JANE HAD MADE Idris Huws a coffee before he left.

Greta Wilson and Emyr Rowlands continuing, for now, the work of piecing together their grizzly remains, even down to matching parts of tattoos. Internal organs would have to be matched to their body parts with further, more in-depth tests which would no doubt take days to complete and confirm.

Greta suspected one might well be female due to the hairless appearance of the skin surface, however, Rowlands commented that he had done enough autopsies on some male bodies which were equally hairless, and seen a few hairy women!

Huws was half promised that with some luck there would be more information within the week.

Jane had told him firmly to come to her home for a decent meal that evening when he declared that he could not in fact really remember when he had last eaten.

"I thought you looked pasty." She had announced.

"Be there for half-six, that gives you plenty of time to get today's tasks out of the way."

"Yes, thank you. You are right, with any luck we will have found our man by then too. He can stew overnight in a cell if needs to, though that is another interview that we won't look forward to."

"Quite right, and you can enjoy a homemade Moroccan lamb stew with me."

Jane winked at him. Idris Huws had no idea what a Moroccan stew consisted of, he simply smiled and nodded his head. Part of him not looking forwards to any stew after what he had seen on the tables that morning.

Huws arrived back at the incident room to find it worryingly quiet, a couple of officers busy typing on their PCs another coming out of the little kitchen three coffees on a tray.

"Can I make you one Sir? We're just getting information through on the Littleton case. A DS from East division has been to interview him this morning, we told him you were currently otherwise engaged and that Rogers, Edwards, and Howard were tied up with the search for Evans. His statement should come through shortly, but, he has definitely coughed to murdering all of them one way or another. No one there in the prison knows why he had this sudden change of heart. He admitted to having stored a considerable stash of drugs too, somewhere near Penmon where he hid out, we are just waiting for a half-decent 1 grid location, as he barely remembered the detail, saying it was dark and the area was unfamiliar, he did say tunnels that were full of cows."

"I have an inkling that I know where Littleton is referring to. I bet you anything someone has threatened him, and he has told them he has a drugs stash. He is so bloody greedy no doubt that if he is going down for four more murders, he doesn't want another scumbag like himself to find the drugs. I will sort that out in a moment too. Let's just get the statement read first but before that I'd definitely appreciate that offer of a coffee."

He had not corrected the officer regarding Justin's whereabouts, which could wait until later.

Chapter Forty-Seven

ROGERS AND EDWARDS, having cleaned up Justin's home, made their way back towards the village of Allt Goch. The search was coming to its end in the immediate area now, all places thought possible, at the distance a man of his age could cover, were well covered.

They had decided between them to go and have a last look at the farmstead if nothing else to check it had been secured after SOCO's had finished there the day before.

The drive was no less potholed as they crept slowly along, meandering their way left and right avoiding the deepest craters. Edwards had lifted the blue tape at the entrance of the courtyard in order that Rogers could drive the car underneath.

"This place gives me the creeps," declared Rogers.

"There are places like this everywhere, people who have continued a family tradition and not been able to move on with modern life and changes in the farming industry. It gets away from them and leaves them behind to scrape a pittance of a living. Why do you think my father and I have an interest in vintage machinery and vehicles? There are still sheds full of them all over the island." Edwards was already making his way towards the door of the house that faced the yard. A window on either side, mainly glassless.

"How do people live like this?"

"By murdering random strangers and eating them apparently. Were there not other serial killers who were cannibals?" Edwards was clearly racking his brain to recollect in order to impress his colleague.

Rogers was less enthusiastic. "I'm sure you can Google that when you get home.

Edwards was reaching forwards for the fingerprint powder-caked doorknob. He paused and took a pair of nitrile gloves from his pocket.

"I know they have finished here but, you know just in case."

"Shush." Said Rogers, tugging at Edwards' sleeve pulling him back. "Did you hear that? I'm sure I heard a cough from inside," she half-whispered. She was already drawing Edwards away from the windows and back into the shadow of the nearest barn.

"Radio this in, we need to get a firearms team here. I'm sure he is inside. I can't imagine it will be anyone else."

Edwards was already talking into his radio, hand shielding his mouth, face turned away from the direction of the door. He listened intently, his earpiece muting the sound of the POLSAR leader receiving his message.

"He has told us to get away to a safe distance and keep out of sight and sound. They are going to send a team of firearms officers as quickly as they can." Edwards had already grabbed Rogers's sleeve as if she were an unruly child.

They walked briskly to the car and reversed just far enough that the car could not be seen from the house.

"I wonder if it is him, maybe it's just local opportunists just having a look, even those so-called Urban explorers that you see on Facebook." Rogers was always full of way-out ideas as far as Edwards was concerned.

In Llangefni, Huws's phone vibrated in his pocket, he dug it out. Edwards name. He answered, to be told that they believed their killer may well have made his way home and could be in the house at this very minute. He was informed that the firearms team had been called out by the POLSAR chief and were on their way.

"Oh Christ, you make sure you both stay out of harm's way."

His blood ran suddenly cold as the vision of the incident at Penmon flashed in front of his eyes, he certainly didn't want another Steffan Parry incident on his hands. Apart from anything else the Chief would have a field day and wipe the floor with him.

He was assured they would keep their heads down. Hopefully, if it was Evans, he would stay indoors.

This was likely to run on into another long day, he remembered his promise to Jane. He should ring her to let her know he was tied up for the foreseeable.

"You just turn up when you are done, whether it's eight, ten or midnight, I'm going to make sure you get some food inside you this evening, or you won't be fit for anything. You can't just keep eating garage snacks."

He agreed.

"Oh, while you are on the phone, did you know that no one had claimed Ashley Evans's body, as in neither his father nor indeed his mother has claimed it for burial. I think the hospital trust will no doubt get the local authority to give them a basic burial. Normally the bodies are only kept for around three months. The only reason this one was kept a little longer is that it was as a result of a crime."

Huws pondered his answer. "Uh, no, it's not something really that I had thought of, but can we hang fire a little time longer? Only because of his relationship with our current fugitive."

"Fair enough," responded Jane. "We're finishing off here shortly, but Emyr and Greta have worked tirelessly through the day. The autopsy room looks like a scene from a horror film, they have managed to piece together the remnants of four bodies for definite, well three if you don't count the dog. The DNA test results were being caught up with this afternoon, we have matched one body to our recent quarry victim, the second to the skeletal remains found by the kayakers, he was the lad missing from Barmouth. The third we're not making much headway with but both Greta and Emyr believe the body parts are female. That one will take a lot more work."

Idris Huws, thanked Jane, assuring her that he would do his best to join her later that night. He needed to make his ways now to Allt Goch and the farm above the shore to join his colleagues. He hoped they would have their man shortly after dusk at the latest.

"Idris, take care won't you, my love?"

Huws, slightly caught out by the term of endearment, assured her he would.

Chapter Forty-Eight

THE FIREARMS TEAM had made their way down the drive, choosing to walk instead of driving down in their vehicles. They aimed to encircle the house using the buildings and nearby hedgerows to get as close as possible. All the chatter was via the radio earpieces.

"I can't see a thing through any of the windows, they're covered in grime," declared one officer, "I need to be able to get a closer vantage point. I'm aiming to try to get to the window to the right of the back door, keep me covered. Notify me if any of you see any movement at all from inside the house, upstairs or downstairs."

"Right, Sir, Thompson has managed to get onto the lean-to roof and is slowly making his way towards the smaller upstairs window."

"Thanks. Thompson, stay alert, this man is capable of anything."

Huws arrived and stopped next to Rogers and Edwards.

"Anything happening?" he asked.

"Not yet Guv, the team is just getting into position. I've just spoken to the team leader, she aims to surround the house first to cover the two exits, she was quite clear that she didn't want any other officers anywhere near the place. Once they are in place, they will ram the door, though, by the look of it, it won't take much breaking.

Huws got into the back of the car and settled down to watch the proceedings, well as far as they could considering they had no view of the house.

Pauline Foster the firearms team commander was just lifting a loudhailer to her mouth when the door facing her opened.

The bumbling dishevelled figure came out, hands aloft. Blinking in the late afternoon low sun, having emerged from the dark of his hovel.

"Get on the floor now," Foster demanded.

William Evans obeyed immediately, if not clumsily and a tad slow. He lay flat with both his hands behind his head. Face to the side, watching a nearby armed officer stride towards him, gun firmly aimed at Evans's head.

"He's out Guv," shouted Rogers, despite Huws only being directly behind her.

Huws and Edwards were already halfway out of the car. She swiftly followed, not wanting to miss out on any detail.

Shortly, William Evans was being half helped, half dragged to his feet by two officers, both having slung their gun harnesses over their shoulders.

Huws could see the old man was smiling. Why the hell would he be smiling after what he had been up to? God only knew how many victims he had placed in that freezer.

Evans was being placed in the back of a squad car, separated from the driver and his colleague by a strong Perspex divider which was a blessing because it was pretty apparent to anyone who stood near enough that he had the smell of an over-ripe muck heap around him.

The only positive was the fact that his clothes were reasonably new, courtesy of his latest victim Simon Chatterris.

The scene was cleared quickly after Evans's removal, Huws just taking a brief look around the house, lest they had missed anything obvious. The house would be secured for the night, the job of keeping it secure allocated to the same two unfortunate officers who had chosen to fall asleep at their recent job at the quarry. They would no doubt never repeat that mistake.

"Get home and try to get a decent night's kip." Ordered Huws of his young team colleagues.

"We have a busy day ahead of us tomorrow."

He walked towards his own car, dialling the direct number of the ward where hopefully Justin Howard was slowly recovering.

Happy with the latest hospital update report he made his way over towards Jane's. She would no doubt let him have a shower before supper. He was certainly looking forwards to a decent meal, good company and maybe if they could switch off from the job, enjoy a film. Netflix was another modern touch that Jane Mathews had introduced him too.

Chapter Forty-Nine

AT THE STATION, a surprisingly meek mannered William Evans was agreeable to all the demands made upon him. The Custody Sergeant as well as the two officers who had bought him in were surprised that this man was capable of doing what he was purported to have done.

He had been read his rights, then the forensics evidence had been gathered, he was stripped of his victim's clothing which was bagged up and labelled, dressed in grey tracksuit bottoms and top which hung off his body. He sat quietly whilst he had his fingerprints taken, his fingernails- as tough as cement were clipped, each piece at risk of flying off in various directions had one officer not shielded the proceedings with an A4 notebook.

They even swabbed his hands and face and saved the potential evidence, individually named in their plastic tubes.

Throughout this procedure, the plan for the next few hours was explained to Evans, he occasionally nodded to show his understanding.

A duty solicitor had been called, Evans claimed that he had never had the need to use the services of such a person.

The plan was to allow Evans to speak to the solicitor in private in a room set aside just for this purpose.

It would be relatively informal, both parties being given a hot drink of their choice.

Evans would be given the opportunity to give his side of the story and be told exactly what would happen lest he had not fully absorbed all the information thrown at him in the initial hour in the custody suite.

He walked off up the corridor between his solicitor and an officer like a little boy going to school.

"Would you ever believe that he had done what he has?" asked the second officer of his colleague.

"Mm, you never know the truth behind some people, never believe what's on the surface."

"Yes, I get that but you wouldn't think of it from an old man like that would you?"

"Hah, you wouldn't believe how many so-called innocent-looking people I have met in this job over twenty years that turn out to be pure evil. I would very much suspect that the old man is the same. Trouble is it makes you not really trust anyone you meet in life. That aspect is not always good."

The younger officer nodded in agreement, though he personally had not yet met many serial killers, and had never realistically expected to meet many in this part of the world.

"Go and get us both a coffee, we may be in for a long night if the DI intends to interview him late this evening." The Custody Sergeant was just finishing off inputting the data, the bags of evidence on the desk ready for delivery to the forensics unit.

"I'm not sure the DI intended to interview him tonight, as far as I know he has gone home. I think he has also sent his senior team home too, probably best when fresh in the morning."

"Hm, will see how things pan out after the solicitor has spoken to him. I don't think it is a good idea personally to leave them to stew overnight and work out their story before the interview."

A slight kerfuffle could be heard up the corridor, looking towards the noise it was apparent that the solicitor had finished. The officer who had been standing guard outside the door was almost knocked over so was the ferocity of the solicitor opening the door.

"He can go to his cell now, he is in no fit state for the interview tonight, I will be back first thing tomorrow."

And with a draught blowing towards the desk from the sudden exit of the solicitor, the two officers just stared at each other.

"What the hell was that about," asked the Sergeant of the officer who was now stepping towards them having just placed Evans in the cell.

"No idea, but he asked us to make sure that Evans had a decent meal inside him this evening, shall I pop out and get him something? He says he is hungry."

Chapter Fifty

HUWS HAD THOROUGHLY ENJOYED his Moroccan stew, or Tagine as Jane had described it, the lamb melting in his mouth. She had followed this up with a home-made lemon meringue pie.

He had made an effort to watch a couple of television programmes as Jane tidied away in the kitchen. He had to his credit offered to help, but she had ushered him into the lounge a second glass of Shiraz in his hand.

Jane had eventually joined him on the sofa. Idris had attempted to stay awake through News at Ten but was struggling.

"Come on, you can't drive home when you're this tired."

Jane took his hand and made to encourage him off the sofa.

"You can stay here tonight."

"No, no honestly, I'll be fine."

Jane insisted, "Go on, you get off to bed, I'll just tidy up in here."

More than likely she was sparing his blushes, not forgetting her own. He could get in bed before she joined him.

This was not necessarily what she had planned, but they were two grown-ups with no ties. It was a long time since she had a relationship, though in reality there had only been two.

Her next decision was a huge step for her, unsure in fact whether she wanted to tie herself to another at her age and stage in life. Used as she was now to doing exactly what she wanted and when she chose to do it. But she liked Idris; he was a kind man. It was difficult for him too, she knew, it wasn't long still since Gwen had died.

She washed the wine glasses and left them till morning on the draining board.

She felt a little like a teenager about to embark on a deeper relationship for the first time. Shy, knowing she had looked after herself, but certainly not a teenage Venus, mind you she reminded herself Idris was likely no longer an Adonis either.

This made her giggle to herself, she made her way to the bottom of the stairs, listening for sounds from above. Only silence.

She found one of her better nighties in the airing cupboard, she would be mortified if he saw her in her usual boring pyjamas.

She jumped in the shower, dried her hair, then entered the bedroom. Idris was asleep, she wanted to giggle again, he was on her side of the bed. Would she feel odd on the wrong side?

She slipped quietly under the covers. Making herself comfortable, making every effort not to wake Idris. Was he a snorer? Mind you did she herself snore? These could only be the thoughts of an older couple. No one really worried about things like that when they were young.

She turned sideways towards Idris, he was naked, obviously, he had no pyjamas. He smelt of her nice shower gel. She placed her arm over his back, he grunted but took her hand and pulled it in closer to his chest. They both fell asleep in this position until the early hours. Idris stirred as if realising for the first time that someone was in his bed. He turned to face a slowly waking Jane.

In the warmth of half-sleep, Idris made love to Jane. None of the frenzied gymnastics of youth. Slow, tender, careful, a tad nervous but deeply satisfying for them both.

Jane lay in Idris's arm, neither of them speaking. Jane fully understanding that this would have been a huge step for Idris. As she turned towards him she saw a tear running down his cheek. She hugged herself closer to him. She guessed exactly what he was thinking.

"Idris, I'm sorry if I steamrolled you rather into staying here last night. Honestly, I don't want to put any pressure on you."

She paused, "I know it's still such a short time since Gwen died, but-"

Idris placed the tip of his finger onto her lips, "Shh, it's fine, honestly, I was just thinking that Gwen would be pleased that I have found someone I can be happy with, that is if you are prepared to take on a curmudgeonly unfit retired detective."

"Curmudgeonly, I can change, unfit, we can work on, retired? Not yet. You have this one case to close, then yes, you can retire. I may just join you in that way too, I am ready now to have a bit of life having worked so hard. I see death every day, I want us to have some good times together before we become too old."

Idris had not felt this content for as long as he could remember since Gwen's passing.

He kissed Jane tenderly, they slowly and tenderly made love once more before the demands of being at work insisted that they got up.

They breakfasted, looking across at Bangor Pier. Que's sera, sera played quietly in the background. They said their goodbyes with a kiss. "See you tonight after work?" asked Jane. Idris responded with a smile and a nod. A smile that Jane had not seen for a long time.

Idris Huws, had a spring in his step that morning as he walked towards his car. His phone rang as he put the key in the ignition. Rogers.

"Morning Sir, just to say, I have just phoned the hospital, Justin is doing well, they let me talk to him this morning. I hope I've not done wrong but I told him all about Littleton admitting the murders. I think he is happy about that. Difficult to tell with him really. I suppose at the end of the day it won't bring Steffan back to him, but he at least now knows that justice will be done and Littleton won't see the light of day ever again. He said that it is likely that he will be discharged later this afternoon. I told him that either myself or Griff will go to pick him up. No one else at the office knows his whereabouts. They have just been told he has a terrible cold, but a negative PCR test so he will be back in a few days.

I'm at the station now, we will wait for you to arrive then we can prepare our interview with Evans? Apparently, he had a good night's sleep, he could be heard snoring from the foyer of the custody suite. His Solicitor plans to be here in about an hour though he has asked to talk to you first."

"Great job Rachel, I'll be with you soon."

Idris Huws had an enthusiasm about him that morning that had been missing for a long time.

Chapter Fifty-One

HUWS WALKED into the Llangefni station virtually side by side with the solicitor representing Evans. He had known him for years. A genuine man, he had represented many a villain, some cases he won, some he lost.

"Morning Idris, can I have a quiet word in your ear before you plan to see William Evans. I know it may be a little unusual, but I have a few worries that I would like to discuss with you?"

"Of course?" answered Huws. "Follow me to my office."

The solicitor looked quite grey. "Can I get you a coffee?" asked Huws.

"No, no, thank you, I'm fine. I'm not sure I can stomach anything this morning, this case has given me a sleepless night."

"Oh?" responded Huws, slightly surprised.

"Well, I spent a bit of time with our man yesterday evening as you will know. I'm not sure there is actually much point in my defending him."

"Why is that? Do you think we won't be able to get a conviction?"

"No, the opposite, you will definitely get a conviction, he admits to everything and more, he does not seem to see that he had done anything wrong, he sort of sees it as his right to have committed these atrocious acts. He turned my stomach listening to him. He is a total psychopath in the real sense of the word. I doubt very much he will end up in prison?"

"I beg your pardon?" exclaimed Huws, the possibilities now slowly dawning on him.

"You mean he will get away with it on diminished responsibility?"

"Well not exactly get away with it, but he will more than likely live out his life in a modicum of comfort in Broadmoor or very likely Ashworth high-security hospital.

I am really not looking forwards to listening to him brag about his killing again today. But I understand I must. I would appreciate though that we maybe have a short break if possible approximately every thirty minutes? I can't see that it will make much difference to the outcome."

Huws was taken aback by the solicitor's openness; it was certainly not the common practice. He was himself now not relishing meeting the man face to face across a table.

Chapter Fifty-Two

HUWS STEPPED into the incident room, a slight feeling of trepidation hanging over him, he was not looking forwards to sitting across the table from their man. He felt different from when he interviewed Littleton, their previous serious case. All he felt then was anger, fury, determination to wipe that sneer off the bastard's face.

This was different. Littleton had at least killed using more conventional methods, God knows what horrors were ahead of them in the next couple of hours. He felt repulsed at the mere thought of talking to such a man.

Rogers and Edwards and the rest of the team looked up expectantly on his entry.

"We have had a pretty prompt match on the clothing belonging to one of our victims." Piped up Edwards, and we will also I believe have a reasonably quick result on any blood evidence that may have still been on Evans's fingernails. Enough to put him away I should think."

Huws nodded.

"I believe that any evidence we actually have from weapons and the man himself and the contents of his freezer, may well just be in addition to the fact that this man, is actually not going to deny the fact that he committed these crimes."

There was a murmur through the office.

"Griff Edwards, young man, I would like you to accompany me for the interview."

Edwards seemed pleased at this request. Rogers less so. Huws realised this.

He made his choice, not to disregard Rogers but to likely protect her from the atrocities they were going to be a party to, at least in the hearing. The solicitor had warned Huws that their man was in no way shy or defensive in his descriptions.

Within minutes, they were notified that Evans had been taken to the interview room, he was handcuffed to the table. The table and chair in turn screwed to the floor. Many an accused had totally 'lost it' and would have no doubt thrown the room furniture around at the point when they realised the game was up.

Huws and Edwards made their way through. Edwards was slightly nervous, his first 'proper' interview. Rogers had told him to basically keep his trap shut and listen, despite the fact that she herself had been unable to do that herself when she was present with Huws whilst interviewing Littleton. She had so much wanted to slap him. Thankfully she kept her control.

Before they stepped into the lion's den as such, because that is exactly how it felt, they went into the adjoining room. Here they could see their man through the one-way glass. Huws never felt totally at ease doing this. Never quite believing that he could not be seen, particularly when some interviewees appeared to look him straight in the eyes.

He was an ungainly man, chiselled features, quite possibly a looker in his youth. His yellow sallow skin now destroying any handsomeness that may have been present then. Angular and malnourished looking. Huws thinking that clearly, his diet had not provided him with what he may have hoped. He looked calm and relaxed, looking about himself as if savouring a newly decorated room in a house. Even this room, square white painted featureless was a far cry from where he had come. He actually looked as if he was making himself comfortable for the duration. His solicitor sat next to him; he could not have seemed more detached from the situation if he had tried.

They could not put it off anymore, a start had to be made. The joy of the previous eight or so hours now only a dim memory for Huws, this man having managed to suck any happiness out of him before he had even spoken to him. They both entered the room and settled their paperwork and files on the table in front of them. Huws taking off his jacket and laying it over the back of the plastic chair.

"Good morning." Announced Evans.

Huws and Edwards looked at each other, surprised and disturbed in equal measure to their accused's apparent cheerfulness.

They sat down.

"Do you understand fully why you have been arrested and why you are here with us now?"

"Yes, of course. I was careless and was caught."

Huws, never one to be lost for words, paused. He looked Evans fully in the eye.

"How many people have you killed?" In for a penny, in for a pound he thought, may as well do away with any bullshit and get to the facts as quickly as they could.

"Well," Evans seemed thoughtful. Would he deny his acts now?

The three of them were agog with disbelief at his audacity when he appeared to be trying to make a count on his fingers. He had used the fingers of one hand when he spread out his palms and chortled, "Gosh, I forget now, I'm not sure how many altogether. Does it really matter? No one noticed that most of them had gone anyway, they were of no importance."

The solicitor visibly squirmed in his chair, looking across at Huws, shutting his eyes then looking towards heaven. He turned to his client.

"You do not have to tell them this." A statement that he felt he should make as opposed to wanted to make.

"What's the point in not telling them?" demanded Evans with a shrug of his shoulders.

Huws bought the situation under control again.

"Let's start with the two recent victims, the young men, one who died in the village the other at the quarry. What do you have to say about that?"

"Wasters." Concluded Evans bluntly. "Just dossers, clearly, no purpose in life. At their ages, going around camping and getting drunk, waste of space, probably a burden on society."

Huws heard Edwards almost whistle as he pushed air out of his lips, he continued.

"Tell us what happened that night."

"Well, yes, that nearly didn't end well for me. One got away, though they say now that he died in the village?"

Huws stared him in the eye.

"I'm not here to fill you in on the details Evans, you are here to tell us what happened that night."

"Yeah well it's, just that he told me that." He indicated towards his solicitor with a shake of his head. The casual attitude belying the true horror.

"Well, I had caught sight of them earlier that day from my front window. I saw them turn off the coast path and go down the new path those footpath people have created down to the quarry. I kept an eye until dusk, but they didn't return, so I assumed they had stayed down there. I packed my bag and started to make my way down there after dark."

"You packed a bag?"

"Yes, just a carrier bag, I took a couple of knives with me, sharp knives. I always made sure I keep them sharpened. You never know when an opportunity arises. Oh, and the pitchfork."

The solicitor had been party to some of this the previous day but not the detail. It shocked him just how casual Evans was in his detailing.

"Carry on," Huws thinking the man was looking at him expecting a prize rosette or similar.

"You walked down there?"

"Yes, I could just about see by moonlight once my eyes had adjusted to the dark, my old eyes are not so good these days, well, in fact most of me is not so good these days" he laughed thinking he had made a joke.

"It's why I took the pitchfork. Thought it best to play it safe and not get too close, what with them being younger an all, no point chancing a knife. I came upon them in the old barracks, they were both in sleeping bags but sitting up chatting leaning against a wall which was lucky for me."

"Lucky? How?"

"Well because they were in sleeping bags, they couldn't use their legs, it was quite funny to see, they were like two kids playing that race that kids play. Now what was it called?"

"The sack race." Edwards butted in.

Huws turned his head, looking at his now blushing junior in disbelief.

"Thank you, Edwards." Just the look told Edwards all he needed to know.

"Go on man, continue."

Evans had thought his last comment amusing, he was still chuckling to himself when he finally composed himself and continued.

"Well, I managed to sneak up to them and took them by surprise in the dark, I got the fork straight into the belly of one of them, he screamed something awful, I hadn't really expected that the fork was sharp enough to go through the sleeping bag but it did. The other one was getting out of his bag at this point, so I swung around and managed to poke him in the guts too, but he managed to leave the building, bloody coward didn't even have the balls to try to help his mate."

He seemed quite pleased with his detailed recollection. No effort at denial, just a sick pride in his achievement.

The solicitor had in fact after this descriptive announcement asked Huws if a short break would be appropriate.

Huws had ignored his plea despite his earlier agreement with him. Evans was on a roll now, better not to stop and risk him changing the story. Part of Huws however, believed that he was revelling in the attention.

"Carry on."

"Uhm well, I had to sort of make a decision on the hoof at that point, I didn't really want the second one to get away, it was too good a chance to miss. I plunged the fork once more into the first guy. I knew I had probably finished him off then because blood was pouring out of his mouth and tummy, you should have seen the look of surprise on his face, he had no idea what had hit him. He didn't move after that, so I went scouting around for the second one. I guessed he would not have gone too far. He was actually just hiding in the bushes at the first bend in the track. I could hear him snivelling and whimpering like a baby."

Evans stopped and looked at the two people staring at him, he looked towards his solicitor as a sort of afterthought. He was occupied wringing his hands together under the desk, his pallor deteriorating by the minute.

Just another couple of minutes thought Huws, then they all needed a breather.

"And then?"

"Well then, I couldn't risk him running off and spoiling things, so I got him a couple more times from the front, he fell over at one point and I managed to get him then too, but bloody hell he must have been tough, he still managed to get up and got away from me. I was not really worried then because I truly believed that he would collapse somewhere nearby and die. I never did get the chance to bother looking for him. I'm quite impressed though that he actually made it up to the village. It must be at least half a mile or so."

The solicitor by now looked deathly pale.

"Right, you are entitled to a short break and some refreshment. What can my officer here get you?"

Huws clearly delegating that job to Edwards, no doubt still dismayed at his childish intrusion.

"I'm fine for the moment thank you very much. I can wait for my lunch, though I do need to relieve myself. My bowels have been giving me gyp this last couple of days, and the fish and chips I was very kindly given yesterday evening is clearly upsetting them."

Huws really did not want to be hearing this. He directed the officers outside the door to accompany Evans to the lavatory but to keep him handcuffed to whichever one of them would draw the short straw. He did not envy them in the least.

Huws and the solicitor went through to his office.

"Sit down," he requested of the by now shaken man.

"If I knew we were not going back into that room, I would offer you a large whisky, unfortunately, that will have to wait. I'll get a coffee bought through for you." He said this as he poked his head out of the glass door and requested two strong coffees. "And not that horrible two in one stuff that you lot drink, use the decent stuff in the cupboard under the sink."

He turned to the solicitor.

"I'll have to find another hidey-hole for my coffee now."

It was pleasing to see the solicitor raise a slight smile at his comment.

"That man is unbelievable, isn't he? The front on him, he does not see anything wrong in what he has done. The murders simply serve a purpose as far as he is concerned. People's lives have no value to him. He has absolutely no remorse. This is the sort of case where the press will have a field day."

Huws fully agreed, but he knew there was a way to go before that stage.

They downed their coffees when they eventually arrived and prepared to return to the interview room.

Chapter Fifty-Three

EVANS once again sat in front of them.

Huws cleared his throat.

"Would you like to continue with what you did in the quarry?"

"Certainly. I made my way back down to the quarry building and the man was obviously dead, so I decided there and then I would try to salvage as much of him as I could while we were undercover. I stripped him of his clothes and stuffed it into the rucksack the other bloke left behind, it looked quite useful. I didn't want the clothes to get too bloody either, because I thought the clothes would do for me, turns out the boots fitted and were really comfortable too."

Huws raised his hand.

"Please get back to facts, it helps no one to go off on a tangent." He said this but knew full well that these tangents simply emphasized the true madness of this man in front of them.

"Sorry." A genuine sounding apology, almost throwing Huws off track himself.

Evans looking thoughtful for a minute, "Right, I think If I remember rightly, I started on his legs, he was quite well-muscled, probably from all the walking, so it was easy enough to strip the meat off the bone, my father taught me butchery skills as a young teenager, we often had the slaughterman visit to dispatch a pig or bullock, pigs were a right pain with having to scrub them with a blade and hot water to remove the coarse hairs and all that saving of blood for the black puddings my mother used to make. Bullocks are much more straightforward.

I carried on, it took a while as I had no light with me, that was a mistake, it would have been easier with a lantern."

Edwards was listening, mouth threatening to drop open. This man in front of them was telling them all this with no feeling of guilt at all. He could not believe what he was hearing. Thank be to God that everything these days was videoed and therefore irrefutable proof of what he had said.

"Once I had stripped off what I could including his liver and heart," he seemed to drift. "My mother used to do a lovely stuffed heart, and come to think of it, my favourite meal of all time was liver, with home-made sausages in a thick onion gravy."

At this point in the proceedings the solicitor asked to be excused, Huws, looking across at him nodded his permission noticing that he was rapidly turning from grey to a distinct shade of green.

"Adrian Roberts, the accused's duty solicitor is momentarily leaving the room."

This was Edwards for the benefit of the recording.

Huws and Edwards looked at each other but stayed silent, knowing they could not continue until he returned. Both hoping they would not be kept waiting for long.

Evans was rubbing his hands together, his cuffs restricting him somewhat.

"How long have you been a policeman?" he asked Huws.

"I quite fancied doing that at one time, but I left school at fourteen to help my parents with all the work."

Idris Huws stared him directly in the eyes. No answer was forthcoming. Thankfully the door was opened from outside to allow Adrian Roberts in, he looked a slightly better colour and came in carrying a tumbler of water.

208

Huws nodded in his direction, an unspoken question as to his condition. A nod was returned.

"Adrian Roberts has returned into the room; the interview will continue." Edwards, feeling pleased to have a job, albeit small to do.

"Please continue Mr. Evans, what happened after you had, in your words, salvaged the flesh off the young man."

"Well, I had done quite a clean job on him really, so I bagged the meat in the plastic bag I had used to carry the knives down, and put the knives in the rucksack."

"Meat?" Huws could not quite contain his anger. "Meat? You call a young man's stripped flesh meat? A young man you had minutes before killed, meat?"

"Well, it was more than a few minutes, because I had need to bleed him, it's not good to not bleed something out before you plan to store meat." Offered Evans in explanation.

Huws shook his head; the solicitor simply hung his. Edwards was now mouth agape, not wanting to believe a word this man was saying, but knowing full well every word was true.

Evans continued. "I'm sorry, I'm upsetting you, it is not intentional. I decided the best thing then was to drag him along the headland to the cliff edge. It was easy to do this now having gotten most of the meat off him. I actually used their tent. I rolled the carcass onto it and it slid quite easily over the ground, then I simply rolled him out of it over the edge of the cliff where the prawns and gulls could feast on the scraps.

I burnt the tent with some matches that were with their gear. It does not do to leave rubbish like that lying around."

Huws was astounded that this man sitting in front of them who had killed what may turn out to be numerous people was concerned about the environment, and unbelievably was apologetic as to his need to describe his actions. He was so phlegmatic, yes that was the word, he had been looking for. Unemotional, calm but Huws knew for certain that there were three people here in this room in the presence of a psychopath. That he was absolutely sure of.

The Solicitor tapped his watch, Idris Huws nodded but continued.

"So, if I am right in my conclusions, are you admitting the murder of Christopher Tennant and Simon Chatterris?"

The old man, seemed hesitant initially, maybe debating internally whether he should admit or not to his crimes. But suddenly- "Yes, I am, my only mistake was to get caught. I obviously did not ask them for their names either."

Adrian Roberts pushed his chair back with some force.

"My client needs a break now, as do we all."

Huws nodded, calling for the officers who stood sentry, they entered, unlocked the cuff attachment from the table-top and took the old man away. Roberts had already pushed his way out past them.

"Jesus." Edwards exhaled as if he might have held his breath through the interview.

"I don't think he played much of a part in this did he." Referring to the Solicitor. Huws shook his head. "We are in the presence of a madman. We have not had too many of these in North Wales, there was that guy Peter Moore in the mid-nineties, I think they got him for the murder of four men, but the belief is that there may have been more. It was believed that his killing spree started on Anglesey."

"Mm, I was around four at the time."

Huws was taken slightly aback by this; in his mind, the eighties were only thirty years ago. Time flies and all that.

"We will let him stew now for a while. I need to just phone the forensics lab just to confirm their findings. We still ideally need to know who all the bodies in the freezer belong to."

Chapter Fifty-Four

THE THREE MEN retreated to Huws's office, sitting down uninvited, the Solicitor put his head in his hands.

"How on earth can I defend that creature, that monster? I have met some bad pennies in my time and thankfully despite my best efforts, the prosecuting barristers and juries have seen the truth and those people have gone down. I have absolutely no evidence which allows me to defend him, and clearly, he is just going to admit to all of his wrongdoing."

Huws simply nodded and poured the man a whisky. Looking across at Edwards, "I won't give you a whisky, you need to get over to the Hospital to pick up Justin."

"Right, you are Sir. Do I take him home?"

. . .

"Well take him home so he can change and have a shower, but if he seems up for it, bring him over for the afternoon, throw him a little into the thick of it, I think it will actually do him better than stewing at home."

"Good idea, yes, I'll see how he is."

Griff Edwards left the two men to their talk, he would log out a car and make his way to Bangor, but not before he had found Rogers and filled her in on the details of the interview.

Adrian Roberts agreed to return to the station at six pm to further interview the prisoner for another couple of hours. He was not anticipating it being any less shocking than the morning session had been.

Idris Huws thanked him and before the emotionally wilting man was even out of the door, he was on the phone to Greta Wilson.

Almost an hour later with the promise that all he had been told had been attached to an e-mail, he had learned that one of the bodies, well, remains of had definitely been connected to the young missing person found on the beach by the kayakers, at least what was left of him.

One selection of contents was confirmed as definitely a dog. Greta reckoned initially that maybe Evans had run low on supplies at this point and either killed his own dog or a wandering stray, or it may have died of old age. The flesh indicated it could well have been an older animal. She added that she had asked the opinion of one of the very experienced senior vet in a local practice to help her on that one, knowing him, she trusted him not to give out details.

· · ·

Quite horrifically, there were frozen maggots within the canine flesh which indicated it may well have lain dead for a while before butchering. Did the man have a tiny bit of empathy, had he cared for the dog, hesitated, and then chosen to do the butchering anyway?

The third body was as yet unidentified though thought to maybe be female, and unbelievingly there were two portions of what appeared to be expertly rolled thigh meat that did not belong to the other portions. Was this a fourth human body?

Greta Wilson continued that the flesh she believed was female appeared to have been stored for a long time, the flesh despite freezing having deteriorated. Had it been pork or beef it would have been binned. Most people she reckoned had that bit of something at the bottom of a freezer that had been overlooked for whatever reason.

Huws had listened to all of this as if in a trance. Not just because of the horror of its telling but the fact that he had sat for over two hours in front of this man who, if showered and shaved and put in a suit, could pass for a regular decent Chapel or Church goer. There was also the fact that Greta Wilson had barely paused for breath as she spoke. Much of the haughtiness seeming to have disappeared from her spoken demeanour.

"Great work, I'll read it all again when the document comes through, it will also guide me a little through this evening's interview when we have all had the chance to compose ourselves. I think the Solicitor will have a nervous breakdown if we try to get back in there too quickly."

. . .

"The document should already be with you, I sent it at soon as I had written up all my findings."

Huws thanked her, ended the call, and immediately sent a text to Jane, knowing better than to phone her at work. Notifying her that he had the interview starting at six but hoped to see her later that evening.

He was surprised to receive an answer immediately, she must have been having a break.

'Looking forwards to it xx' Idris Huws smiled to himself. He felt that something good would come out of this for both of them.

Just as he was putting his phone back in his pocket, young Rogers came in clutching the promised report.

"Have you read it?" he asked her.

"Well, yes, should I not have done?" She sounded wary as if caught out being naughty.

"Of course, you can read it, I also want you to have read the transcript of this morning's interview too, you quite honestly won't believe what you are reading. That man is unbelievable. If I was not sitting right there opposite him, I would be persuaded that I was reading the script of a pretty gruesome horror film. That man will be put away for a very long time."

. . .

"Griff told me had spent the morning sat opposite a real-life mad man, the stuff of nightmares."

Huws nodded. "He has. I've sent him to pick up Justin now. I have no idea if he has actually been discharged yet, but Griff will be a friendly face when he is allowed out. Rightly or wrongly, he I told him to take him home for a shower then bring him here later this afternoon." He paused momentarily. "I assume the rest of the team have no idea what has been going on? That is to be kept between the four of us?"

Rogers nodded.

"No one knows. As you say, it is for the best."

She turned on her heels then stopped in her tracks.

"Oh, and Guv, there is a whip-round in the office, they have organized a collection to have a little 'do' here in the office at the end of this case when you said you were going to be retiring? Are you still planning to retire? We generally decided that you would want it kept low key, and we have not bothered organizing a venue because of the Pfaff with Covid passports and all that. We have asked a few extra people if they would like to attend, you know Emyr Rowlands, Jane, and the DCI."

She waited for his reaction.

. . .

"Lovely yes, just low key though please, I don't want a fuss and don't want it to get messy. In answer to the retirement question yes I will be relinquishing the reins. I've spoken at length to DCI Williams, and we believe that DS Howard will make a splendid DI. Edwards will be promoted to DS and you young Rogers will become a Detective Constable, so a jump into Civvies for you."

"Oh God, that will cost me a fortune in new clothes!" this was followed by a guffaw of laughter. "Only joking Guv, thank you for recommending me."

She almost floated out of the room.

Huws felt they all needed a bit of lightness at the moment when enveloped by such a cloak of evil darkness.

Chapter Fifty-Five

THE AFTERNOON HAD PASSED RELATIVELY QUIETLY. Evans had been given his lunch for which he thanked the young PC graciously for its delivery. He asked if he could have a suitable cloth to form a bib. The young policeman simply stared at him mouth open not believing his audacity. He slammed the cell door shut with a little more ferocity than was truly necessary.

Huws had thoroughly read and caught up with the paperwork, but best of all at four-thirty Edwards had walked into the incident room followed by a still pale-looking Justin Howard.

There were calls of "OK mate, feeling better?" from various corners of the office. Justin confirmed his state of health with a thumbs up. He went immediately to his desk. Rogers suggested to him that he caught up on the recent developments with William Evans. He agreed and accessed the relevant documents.

At precisely ten minutes to six, Adrian Roberts' knuckle tapped Idris Huws's door.

"Come in, are you OK? You are a little pinker around the gills now than you were when you left this morning. Now I know it certainly is not the done- thing, but we all know where this case is going. I'm offering you the opportunity before we get Evans in the interview room for you to have a read of the Forensic report that arrived this morning. It may be fairer to you to be prepared for anything we hear this evening.

This suggestion was received gratefully. He took the typed-out document from Huws and had a brief look through it.

"Mm well, beyond belief isn't it? Who do you reckon the female might be?"

"We have not delved into that at all yet, we were maybe hoping that his openness to describe his acts may just reveal that as a matter of course. If he does not tell us, then that will simply mean we have to look into it further though I do know and you will read it on the report that they are awaiting DNA results on both the suspected female body parts and the small number of other unidentified body parts that were towards the bottom of the freezer. They will try to match it will our existing DNA database. The team next door is also going through old missing persons reports from up to thirty years ago. The meat at the bottom of the freezer is thought to have a fair age to it."

Adrian Roberts, spent a couple more minutes in silence reading the document before handing it back to Huws and standing up. He picked up his old slightly battered leather briefcase and made to follow Huws through. He could be heard taking a deep inhalation of breath.

"Poor Man," was Huws's thought.

Evans was sitting relaxed at the desk. Evidence of food stains down his tracksuit front.

"Apologies for the state of my top, but I did ask for a bib, my teeth are not the best these days."

He even drew back his lips exposing tombstone-stained teeth. It almost turned Huws's stomach. This man was unbelievable.

Edwards had entered the room. He switched on the recording device, described who were present in the room before Huws began.

"Right, can we continue from where we left this morning? Can you tell us about the other bodies in the freezer?"

Before Huws had barely finished the request, Evans explained that one of them was the man he had come across in the quarry, likely a junkie, he did not think anyone would miss him. He had enjoyed some portions of the young man but had been put off slightly by the tattoos on his skin, his arms and back had been totally covered by ink, it had slightly made him queasy, it made the skin look mouldy. He had chosen to keep him for the future if he ran short."

Huws shook his head at this explanation, disbelief unable to be disguised.

"And the other portions, at least two more human bodies and a dog?"

For the first time, Evans hesitated, he looked thoughtful, he put his head down towards his hands, his attempt to grasp his head. He was silent. Huws did not push him at this point.

Evans looked up and a tear was spilling over his reddened eyelid, slowly running down his cheek.

"Sweep. He was jet black all over, unusual for a collie, a good dog, didn't have much use for him after the sheep went, but he was a half-decent ratter. He kept their numbers down if I kept him a little tight for food."

At this point Huws wanted to scream at the man, unbelievably he had discussed with them in lurid detail his ability to heartlessly murder at least three people they knew about, and here he was shedding a tear about a dog.

"Did you intentionally kill the dog?" This was Edwards.

"Of course, I didn't, why would I kill the dog? He died." He paused as if to plan his answer.

"I found him dead curled up in his kennel, he might have been dead a couple of days because he'd not eaten the scraps I had thrown him, he usually enjoyed those scraps."

"Scraps?" Edwards again.

"Gristle, sinew, you know bits that I could not chew with these." He pointed again at his teeth.

Edwards was exhaling slowly and deeply, trying hard not to let rip totally at this monster in the room.

I decided that I might as well skin him and joint him, maybe if I ran short I could maybe use him then. That was hard, it made me sad he was a good dog in his youth."

At this point Evans became silent, eyes closed looked towards the ceiling.

Was this going to become an outpouring of remorse?

Edwards phone pinged. He looked at the screen he slipped Huws a hastily scribbled note. He wanted to just pop out for a few moments, he had something he needed to do. Five minutes was all he needed.

Huws chose to continue the interview alone.

The other bodies?"

"Mm, there was a man, he trespassed on my land, but that was a long time ago, I forget exactly the detail. He wasn't the first. Probably nothing left of him now."

There were more! thought Idris Huws to himself. Unbelievable. He would pursue this first whilst Evans was in the flow.

"How many more? Can you at least tell us that?"

"Three, four? I can't fully remember. Waifs and strays mainly, but they have all gone now."

"All gone?" Huws really did not want to hear this.

"Yes, all gone."

"Where to?" Huws knew exactly what this answer would be, it had to be asked. It was clear to Idris Huws that the solicitor was taking on a slightly green hue again, just like the morning.

"Gone, as in cooked, the dog and myself have eaten them, the dog really enjoyed his scraps." He repeated this statement as if partly blaming the dog's need for food as being the cause of this terrible heartless cannibalism.

Edwards returned to the room. He passed Huws a note.

Ask him when his mother died.

A single line.

Huws looked across at Edwards, he nodded.

"Evans, can you tell me when your mother died?"

Evans looked slightly taken aback but seemed to compose himself pretty quickly.

"Yes, bless her, she died in September nineteen eighty-nine. Why do you ask?"

"I ask the questions here; can you tell me where she was buried?"

"Oh, she wasn't buried, she asked for cremation, my father was cremated. She wanted the same." Evans seemed quite confident again.

"Where were her ashes buried or spread?" A random question that in the grand scheme of things did not seem important but Huws asked it nevertheless.

This seemed to have taken the wind slightly out of Evans's sails for a moment.

"Uhm, oh, if I remember rightly Bangor Crem."

"If you remember? Surely you will remember where you cremated your mother?"

Huws was on a bit of a roll. He sensed that Evans was behaving a little like a cornered rat.

"Yes, yes, it was Bangor, she had cancer I think. It upset me terribly."

Huws came back at him again, louder this time.

"You think? Good God, you must remember what she died of, you must have cared for her? Doctors must have visited her? There must have been a death certificate issued when she passed. Did she pass away at home or in the hospital? Was there an autopsy or was the cause of death put down as a type of cancer?"

William Evans seemed momentarily shocked at this bombard-ment of questions. He sat back and looked Huws straight in the eye.

"Yes, well she died at home."

"What Doctor or Doctors treated her?"

"I forget, there were a few."

Huws shut his file abruptly and stood up. "Door." He said, a little louder than necessary.

The two officers stepped in.

"That will be all for tonight. Feed him, we will continue tomorrow."

"Thank you." Uttered Evans as if they were doing him a great kindness.

Edwards, Huws and the grey-looking Solicitor, picked up all their paperwork and once again made their way to the office.

"What was that all about Edwards?" Huws turned to the DC.

"Rogers messaged me. There has been a development regarding the third body, the one at the bottom of the freezer. It's likely to be the case with the other unknown unestablished portions too. We have a DNA match."

"God, how did that come about?"

"Well, Emyr Rowlands apparently suggested to Greta Wilson that she compared the meat DNA to Ashley Evans, William Evans' son. They have it recorded, mind you, he is still in the mortuary awaiting burial by the council."

"And?"

Both Huws and the Solicitor sat agog.

"Ashley Evans's DNA is an extraordinarily close match to the body in the fridge. They are just going to double-check the results from the spare portions now."

Huws shook his head as if dislodging an irritating fly.

"So, are you telling me then, that it is therefore likely that William Evans's DNA will also be a close match, as in a family tie?"

"Looks a possibility, yes." Edwards shivered as if cold.

"Okay, let's leave them to get on with their work. We need to plan this carefully. Let him stew in there for a night. He is probably having a better time in that cell than he has enjoyed for years. We can all sleep on it. Tell Rogers that I want you, Justin, and herself to do a thorough check tomorrow, contact the local registrar. I know the office has moved to Llangefni, but all the death registrations will still be on a database. Start with nineteen eighty-five to allow for his error. I need to know when his parents died, what they died of, and where they were buried. I will interview him again at ten am. I need to just OK it to keep him longer, though having admitted to the other murders, it is not an issue. Get a good night's sleep. I will see you both in the morning."

A nod towards the Solicitor saw his agreement to the request.

Chapter Fifty-Six

IDRIS SAT in his car outside the station. For a few moments, he wanted to be by himself. The information that he had gleaned over the last barely twenty-four hours was both horrific and unbelievable in equal measures. If someone gave him a shove now and he realised it had all been a dream, he could well believe it. He looked at his watch and started the engine. Part of him was tempted to drive back to his own house to spend the evening alone, the other part of him did not want such solitude. He needed to be with someone.

He set off out of the county town, choosing the cross-country route towards Beaumaris, taking his time, realising after twenty minutes that he had no recollection of actually driving through Pentraeth, or Llansadwrn come to that.

He dropped down into Beaumaris, there were more people around now. Everywhere waking up it seemed after a long winter where Coronavirus had been to the forefront of most people's minds. It had not gone away according to the daily figures but complacency was creeping in slowly but surely.

He parked up across Jane's garage door, knowing she would be home already and would not need her car until the morning.

She met him at the front door, stepping towards him, offering him a hug.

"You've had a rough day, I should imagine, but you know, in my house today, you will leave work outside the door, it will be waiting patiently for you there in the morning. Come on, go through into the lounge and sit down. Take your shoes off. Supper won't be long."

That night was long and sleepless for Idris. His mind replayed the interview over and over. Normally he would be pulling all the information apart, word for word, trying to see if he could catch the suspect out with a lie, or an incorrect repeat of information. This was totally different; no denials were being made. Evans seemed happy to disclose everything he had done. He actually appeared proud of an achievement.

He had apologised to Jane when they got into her bed.

"It will be a poor show, tonight love, I'm exhausted. Can we just enjoy a hug and a cuddle? I know it is not how normal second dates go, but, do you mind?"

Her response had made him laugh at least.

"Thank be to God, I'm too old to be with a twice a night man now, being menopausal and all that. I was wondering what vitamins I should take to keep up with you."

They spooned together, finding comfort in each other's familiarity. They fell asleep, Idris holding Jane tightly about the waist.

Tomorrow was another day.

Chapter Fifty-Seven

WILLIAM EVANS again for a second night, slept the sleep of a contented man, much to the annoyance of the custody officers doing the late shift. He could be heard snoring and grunting from way down the corridor.

Chapter Fifty-Eight

THE TEAM WERE in the incident room bright and early. Long before their superior had risen and breakfasted. Though up to now they were totally unaware of any developments in his love life. Thankfully, he was certain he would be a butt of their jokes.

Justin, seemingly more refreshed and content. Had ridden in with Edwards that morning. Huws would speak to him later in privacy, he did not want to arouse any suspicion regarding the young officer's absence.

Rogers had written out their tasks on the Perspex board.

There were a few urgent phone calls to make that morning. Rogers having already contacted the Council Senior Registrar to be told that they were mainly working from home, but the very kind lady had offered to drive to her office in order to be able to check the archive via the database.

She had promised to call back immediately once she had the information that the team needed.

They were waiting with bated breath.

Edwards was busy writing down some headings, likely he would not get invited to ask questions, but it may help himself and the DI to continue a logical path of questioning. The duty solicitor was sitting on the plastic seats in the corridor. Not once thought Edwards, had he advised his client to not answer a question.

If today went to plan, though he was not sure of the exact plan, no doubt Evans would be appearing in court the following day. He would be charged and would appear in court for a trial in the very near future. Edwards believed this as there was no actual defence in place. The Prosecution would have a field day.

"I certainly hope the jury have a strong stomach." Announced Edwards to no one in particular, just voicing his thoughts.

"Was it truly awful listening to the old man?" Rogers had been slightly envious, however having heard snippets of the interview from Edwards she was secretly quite pleased not to have been party to it. She had fetched the solicitor a glass of water the previous day, he had almost staggered out of the interview suite, she honestly believed that he was going to faint right there in front of her, or vomit, thankfully he had done neither.

"You can't imagine the....." he was cut off mid- sentence. Rogers' phone was ringing, she was writing down whatever she was being told on a notepad, but it didn't look like much. She put her pen down and ended the call.

"Well?" asked Howard. "Any news?"

"You are not going to believe this."

"Go on, what is it? I will believe anything when it comes to that man." pushed Edwards.

"Believe what?" came a voice from the office doorway.

"Oh, morning Guv." Huws stood with an expectant look on his drawn face.

"I have just received a call from the County registrar lady, she kindly went into her office to access the older database on the computer. She says there is no record whatsoever of either of Evans's parents having died, no burial records, no death certificates, nothing at all. She managed to access their birth certificates, their marriage certificates as well as a birth record for both William Evans and his son Ashley, but nothing more. Is that not odd, particularly as his mother was supposedly cremated at Bangor crematorium?"

"Odd, but nothing surprises me about that man. Check up with the crem records. We need to put some real pressure on him today. I believe from a couple of reactions yesterday that his mother may be a subject too far for him. Can we find out from the path lab and forensics just how much of the body is left in the bottom of the freezer?"

Huws requested Rogers to make headway on that point. She was straight on the phone.

Huws went to the kitchen and made a coffee for himself and the Solicitor, still patiently waiting for the nod. He seemed pleased that the ten-o clock interview time had come and gone.

He held the coffee, more warming his hands with the hot cardboard cup than looking as if he would drink its contents.

"We're in for another tough day I believe," voiced the DI.

Andrew Roberts grimaced at this thought.

"Some of the team are still trawling through the National Missing person's database, but in all honesty, I think that is a total waste of time. There is no way we can link anyone to him now, we have no body parts remaining, and we certainly can't accuse him of being responsible for being involved in all of them, there are thousands of them. If we even stuck to locally based ones, we will never find them all. Maybe we can encourage him to divulge his methods. That might be a start. The information we now have on his parents, you will have to wait to hear."

Huws hesitated.

"Good God man, I have no idea why I'm even telling you all this as the defence lawyer. But this seems to be the way it has gone."

Huws, Edwards and Adrian Roberts went into the small adjoining room, they watched their man being bought into the interview room, placid, calm, a picture of quiet anticipation if there was such a description. He sat down and placed both hands before him whilst the officer clipped his handcuffs to the ring on the table. To look at him on a street anywhere, you would never believe that he had been capable of such things.

Not able to put it off any longer, they joined him, taking long moments to arrange their chairs, Huws removing his jacket, placing it carefully over the back of his chair. Edwards was organizing his paperwork in front of him, his quickly scribbled notes hidden by the top sheet, easily retrieved if needed. The Solicitor had not even opened his briefcase, let alone put any case notes on the table.

"Good morning yet again gentlemen."

Evans spoke as if he had randomly met them in a shop.

Huws just could not get his head around the audacity.

He knew by now; a duty psychiatrist would have a big part to play once this stage was complete and he had been officially charged. Huws chose to ignore his comment.

Evans promptly relaxed his midriff and slumped slightly in the chair. He was making himself comfortable for whatever lay ahead. Huws decided to leave the information regarding his parents in the bag as further ammunition.

"How did you entice people into your clutches, surely not everyone trespassed on your land. You must have met some of the others you claim you killed some other way?"

Evans paused for a few moments. Deep in recollection by the way he looked.

"Some of them were just stupid people, they were asking for it, total idiots, their own fault."

This was the first indication of a raised voice. Clearly, Evans was insinuating that there was no blame on his part.

"Go on."

Huws tried to sound encouraging, though it was patently obvious that Evans had no shame or remorse.

"Well at least two of them, offered me a lift when I was walking from town. They would stop, particularly if it was raining. They would bring me home and I would usually offer them a cup of tea or something. They always accepted, stupid people, I took the opportunity to cut their throats from behind as they entered the back door, always told them to go ahead and straight on, they never guessed. I was stronger then and dragged them to the barn where I could hang them for a while before butchering them."

He looked across the table, Huws felt he was expecting a clap, a round of applause.

"So how many exactly, did you dispose of like this?"

"I forget, it was a long time ago, before my mother died, hence not letting them into the house."

"Two, three four?" Edwards butted in, not able to help himself.

"Yes, probably." No reluctance or hesitation in his answer.

"Yes, how many? Two, three, or four?" Edwards again.

Adrian Roberts had a look of total despair on his face.

"Maybe, four, five. It is bound to be clouded in my memory after all this time, I would hate to give you an exact figure and then find I was wrong."

His openness was sickening.

"Do you have no shame man? You have committed the most awful series of murders and you are talking as if you have forgotten how many eggs a hen might have lain."

Huws was close to blowing a gasket, he knew he needed to keep a lid on things.

Evans simply shrugged.

"Sorry, I can't help you more than this, my mind plays tricks on me. My memory isn't what it used to be."

He looked around at the three silent men as if wanting sympathy.

"My father found out though, he came into the barn one day, unexpectedly after he had been to a machine sale. He saw what I was doing, obviously, I could not let him tell my mother. It would have upset her dreadfully. He ran at me to stop me, though it was far too late by then. I had to stop him; he was going mad. He was shouting and raving like a madman."

"Like a madman?" asked Huws, incredulous that this creature sitting no more than four feet away considered his father the mad man.

"Yes, screaming he was at the top of his voice, threatening to phone the police, everything. I had to stop him, I stabbed him. It made my job much harder that day having the two bodies to deal with especially with the freezer being almost full too. But I managed it."

No one spoke, so shocked were they at how cool Evans appeared to be.

Evans unprompted continued, calmer now.

"I had to tell my mother the following day that my father had left her, they were always falling out anyway. It was not rare for him to raise his hand to her either. Quite a nasty man, hiding behind being a lay preacher too. She believed to her dying day that he had simply walked out of our lives."

Huws took the mention of his mother as an opportunity to wade in.

"Tell me again when your mother died?" A command as opposed to an invitation.

"Nineteen eighty-nine." He was subdued at the mention of his mother.

"There is no record of your mother's death. No record of your father's either, but now we know why don't we? Did the same happen to your mother?"

This seemed to enrage the man, the first glimmer of a temper that they had really seen.

"How dare you? I loved my mother, I would have done anything for my mother, of course, I didn't kill her."

"No record of her burial either." Added Edwards. "You lied to us yesterday, you told us she had been cremated in Bangor Crematorium along with your father. That was a blatant lie wasn't it?"

Evans looked at the men around him, tears overspilling his eyes. Only the second intimation of sentiment.

"No comment."

This took the wind totally out of their sails.

"What happened to your mother Evans? Did you kill your mother Abigail Evans, along with your father Thomas Evans?"

The first mention of his parents by their names seemed to catch him out. He squirmed in his chair, sat up again to his full height.

"I did not kill my mother."

"Tell us what happened to your mother then, she must have been so upset that your father had left you both like that. You were also married I believe, to Ashley's mother? That didn't last long did it?" Huws was pushing on now.

"Your son was killed a couple of years ago wasn't he? I dealt

231

with that case. The perpetrator in his case has just admitted guilt to his killing. You chose not to bury your son; he is shortly to be interred at the cost of the council. How do you feel about that?

"No comment."

Not only was Evans agitated now. Adrian Roberts was increasingly twitchy in his seat. He had pulled his notebook out of his briefcase and was now furiously scribbling. The nib of his fountain pen scratched its way across the paper.

This was his worst nightmare. This change in attitude now likely meant he would need to speak to this man again, alone.

"Enough for now, have a serious think about what you are telling us now Evans. We have new information to hand regarding your mother, we will be speaking to you again later."

With much scraping of chairs, they left the accused. Huws could not be more disgusted if he tried. This case would be with him for a very long time.

"Roberts, how do you want to take this forwards now? This next bit is firmly in your hands. We need to know exactly what happened to his mother, facts are very much pointing towards the likelihood that his mother's body, albeit cut into joints as he calls them is lying at the bottom of his freezer."

The gaunt man standing in front of him, his overlarge shirt collar appearing to grow larger every time he turned up, was speechless. Huws felt sympathy towards him. He knew the last place he wanted to be this afternoon was to be alone in the upstairs private interview room with Evans.

"I'll speak to him, I can't promise I will get anywhere as you well know, but I have a request. Can I be sure that there will be an officer available right outside the door and that the suspect will remain cuffed at all times? I hate to think what that man might be capable of if things get heated."

"Of course, I will assure you of that, but please do your best, we need to put this to bed now- for all our sakes. This will live with us for a very long time."

"Thank you DI Huws."

Adrian Roberts slowly made his way towards the stairs. Idris Huws did not envy him one bit. He could sense his reluctance seeping from every pore in his body.

Chapter Fifty-Nine

IDRIS HUWS REJOINED his young team in the incident room, the sudden silence at his appearance instilling a frisson of tension.

The team fully knew that this case was very much coming to its inevitable conclusion.

Justin suddenly raised his hand, indicating that they should be quiet. He continued to listen to his incoming phone call. He shook his head intermittently with an occasional nod.

"The other remains at the bottom of the freezer are almost definitely the father."

"Wow." Rogers was open-mouthed, having not been party yet to the last interview. "He ate his father? That man is a monster."

"State the obvious why don't you?" Called the DC from the back of the room.

"Listening to him today has been like reading a horror book by Stephen King. Not just what he has done, but he seems to think it is normal." Edwards clearly sickened by what he had heard in the last hour.

Huws turned on his heels.

"Adrian Roberts is upstairs with him now. Someone let me know as soon as he has finished. I want this case wrapped up tonight, though, in all honesty, we have plenty to put him away with what we have got. I want as much as we can find, his depravity is just unbelievable. He should never see the light of day."

Chapter Sixty

HUWS AND EDWARDS entered the interview room for what was they hoped, the last time.

Evans was already seated and secured next to Adrian Roberts his solicitor.

The recording devices were swiftly switched on.

"Mr. Evans is fully willing to comply and answer any questions you may have for him."

Huws looked from Roberts to Evans.

"I would certainly hope so. There is nothing to be gained from untruths or denials at this stage."

Evans, eyes red-rimmed nodded his head.

Huws astounded that this man in front of him had clearly been crying, no doubt crocodile tears. It was often the case with men like him.

Thankfully he had not met many psychopaths in his years on the job, but he fully understood that he was more than likely crying at the realization that there was no way out for him now, as opposed to the fact that he felt any remorse whatsoever at his wrongdoing. Huws decided to cut to the chase.

"We have evidence now which is undeniable that the remains

that were in the very bottom of your freezer were those of your mother with just a few body parts left of your father. Did you cook and consume your father?"

He waited for his answer.

"Come on man, have you at some time in the past eaten your father?"

"Yes."

Huws looked across at the ashen solicitor and then at Edwards who had not taken his gaze away from William Evans in front of him. Idris Huws hoped that the young DC would not have to deal with a case like this ever again in his career.

"Did you kill your mother? According to our forensics teams investigation-" He paused. William Evans was staring down at his clasped hands.

"I repeat, did you kill your mother? The forensics team state that in their opinion all of your mother's body parts are likely still intact. You haven't consumed your mother?"

Huws used the word consume, simply as it did not seem to have the same horrific connotation as the word 'eat'.

"No, I did not kill my mother, I would never have killed my mother, I loved my mother." Tears again now. Huws ignored them and ploughed on.

"So much so that you cut her up and stored her in the freezer. Where are the rest of her remains? Her head, her bones?"

Silence, head hung, the arrogance having left him.

"I did not kill her, she died, I cut her up and I burnt her remains. But once done, I just could not bring myself to consume her flesh, even though at the time my supplies were low, most of my father's body had gone. It turned my stomach, I did try, but couldn't. It is why I went looking for others. I think she had cancer, I was afraid I might somehow catch it off her."

Evans allowed a tear to run down his cheek, he gave a huge soggy sniff, wiping the mucus leaving his nose with his sleeve.

Edwards looked away.

"Shit man, you are disgusting."

Huws raised his hand in front of Edwards as if holding back a troublesome puppy.

"How did your mother die?"

Twice more Huws asked the sniffing man in front of him the same question.

Adrian Roberts encouraged him to continue.

Evans looked across at his solicitor, a look of pleading innocence on his face as if hoping his solicitor would cover for all his misdemeanours as if he were simply a first-time burglar.

Huws, repeated his question with a degree of ferocity that belied his usual placid demeanour. It appeared to stir Evans into action.

"She died right there in front of me in the house, there was nothing I could do, I didn't know what to do, but I didn't kill her. My father killed her."

"I beg your pardon." Demanded Huws, this admission had caught him on the back foot.

"Your father was dead years before your mother? How could this be?"

"Yes." He admitted.

"So how did your father killed your mother."

A huge part of Huws didn't to hear the man's answer.

"Tell us, you need to tell us how your mother died."

"She choked. She choked and died there right in front of me. My bloody bastard of a bullying father who beat my mother managed to kill her in the end."

A slow realization came over Huws, Edwards still had a look of surprised expectation on his face. The solicitor was already putting his folder into his briefcase.

"We were eating a stew made of a part of my father when my mother choked."

Evans guffawed a huge gasp of air and howled.

Huws was silent, no words were available or applicable at this juncture.

"Door!" he shouted, immediately the officers entered.

"Take him away, he will be formally charged shortly."

They nodded as they unlocked the cuffs from the table. He was escorted through the door; he could still be heard howling once his cell door had been shut on him.

Evans appeared in court the following day, the case against him to take place in just a few days. He showed no emotion whatsoever, gave his name and address, no hesitation. He seemed to have composed himself from the previous day's burst of what the team believed was false emotion. In the interim time the psych team would endeavour to dig into his persona, no doubt agreeing, as the solicitor had inferred that he would be incarcerated for the duration of his natural life in a secure prison.

Huws and his team spent the next few days in almost a sober silence, collating the evidence, trying to keep the press at bay. This was to be the biggest crime to have taken place in the locality, ever. Despite the fact there had been recent cases in the area, this had the horror aspect that the team hoped they would never witness again.

DI Idris Huws would be present at court for the case, but by the time he would be giving evidence he would be days from retiring permanently. It would likely be the shortest trial in the history of such a serial killer, but having no defence other than his psychological state of mind he would be in a secure unit within days of the appearance. In the short term, he would be imprisoned, with the highest security. In a strange sort of way Huws believed that if the man got three square meals a day then killing would not enter his mind ever again.

DCI Williams had already visited to congratulate the team on its success. A subdued Justin Howard having already accepted the step up to be in a few weeks to DI.

A new and very capable DS would step up to the plate in the secure hands of Griff Edwards, with young PC Rachel Roberts stepping out of uniform into civvies in her new role of Detective Constable. She had certainly proved her worth.

The retirement party after the case was a quiet affair, office-based, amongst friends just as Huws wanted it. Jane at his side and a special invitation having been extended to his old friend Emyr Rowlands, who surprised them all, though no one admitted it, to have bought his new lady friend with him in the name of Greta Wilson.

Huws winked when he welcomed his old friend, happy to receive a bottle of Lagavulin.

"Good of you both to come." Said Huws.

"I would not miss it for the world, and Miss Frosty Knickers was very keen to accompany me today."

Huws felt himself reddening, until they both started laughing. Jane joined them in the hilarity.

"We will miss you Idris, but I'm sure we will keep in touch.

About the Author

A late starter to putting ink to paper. She lives on the Island of Anglesey where she has set her books. She draws on life experiences and interest in all things outdoors as well as some of her voluntary work as a Coastguard officer.

No one in her book is real, all a figment of her imagination, but some of the procedures that take place within the series are based on real methods of rescue.

Also by Anne Roberts

DI HUWS BOOK 1 Community Killings

DI HUWS BOOK 2 Community Secrets and Lies

On the Run- a stand alone short story

Printed in Great Britain
by Amazon

24257249R00139